BLURB

Destiny is blind, unable to see outside his realm. He's bored, lonely, and beginning to dread his duties—until he discovers an unconscious woman on his couch. He has no idea where she came from or how she got there, but he wants to keep her. What lengths is he willing to go to make that happen? Is he willing to enter her world? With his mother determined to have her way, the universe will become the story of what you see isn't always what you get.

Zandra wakes on a couch in the biggest library she has ever seen; she can't remember where she is, how she got there, or even her own name. She is easily distracted by Destiny, the man of her dreams.

DESTINY'S FATE

DUTIFUL GODS

BOOK ONE

MELISSA BELL

EDITOR

MICHELE THOMPSON
Thank you for your patience and hard
work,
in fixing bad grammar and punctuation.
Having you as a friend, I feel blessed.

DEDICATION

Without the love and support of Jordin Thiele, whose encouragement and tolerance helped my words bear fruit. Thank you for reading and re-reading my chapters, so that I could get them just right. I did it.

CHAPTER 1

Glancing in the mirror at her new black cocktail dress and strappy sandals that her boss obviously thought she paid enough to afford, Zandra Wilson pulled loose a couple of wisps of her black hair and muttered to herself, "Good as it's going to get." She snatched her purse off the dresser and made her way to the door. She was already running late; damn, she hated these work parties, even if they did only happen once a year. Considering the day she'd had, this was the last thing she wanted to be doing on a Friday night. Admittedly, she didn't have a choice. Zandra loved her job, but she would have given anything to be doing it for a different boss. Unfortunately, the bully bitch owned the damn company. "Hmm, maybe I'll start looking into that... tomorrow." She laughed at the fact she was starting to sound like the crazy cat lady talking to her ninety-nine beloved pets, "I don't think fluffy slippers count."

She made her way out the door making sure to lock up, while checking to see she had everything needed for the meet and greet - Keys, Phone, Driver's License, Money and Lipstick. Amazed at how much fit into the little clutch purse, she headed to her prized red Audi, the only thing she owned outright as of two months ago. Every time she saw it, she was filled with a sense of accomplishment. It reminded her of the reason why she took her job so seriously.

Friday night should be spent with the girls doing all the usual girl stuff. At thirty-two, she had a well-established girl's night out thing going on. Even when she started seeing Ethan, she had insisted that their

Friday night's stay as their girl's and boy's nights out.

Pulling out of her street she made her way to the party. If traffic permitted she would be there by ten past eight. Still, she would be late in the eyes of her boss. Like really? Did the vulture ever sleep? She supposed that was why her husband worked the night shift - their monies tied up together meant that it was a marriage on paper resembling a one hundred-dollar bill. Foreplay was probably a bidding war. Maybe that was why she was such a cow of a woman, she needed to get laid. She shivered at the direction her thoughts had gone, and not in a good way.

She wondered what tonight would bring, considering her day had been far from perfect. Stopping at the lights, waiting to turn right, she could only reflect on the text message she had received from Ethan this morning.

Her phone rang, drawing her attention back to the here and now. She answered it on her hands free as the light changed to green and the car behind her tooted its horn to as if to say, "Impatient asshole."

"Zandra," said her boss, "Where are you? You're supposed to be here. It's now three minutes to eight, and I needed you here an hour ago."

Zandra replied, "I'm about ten to fifteen minutes away, and the clients aren't scheduled to arrive until eight-thirty. I have plenty of time to be there before them."

"Yes, well, I wanted you here at six-thirty," said Anne. "You know how I dislike it when things are not done the way I want them, and what if there are some last-minute changes I need to make? Who will take care of those?"

Zandra, concentrating on the road answered automatically, "What kind of last-minute changes?" Waiting to hear that all too familiar response.

Anne replied, "Well that's not important now is it? We don't have time to do anything about them."

Zandra knew there were no last-minute changes. It was just her control freak of a boss, trying to monopolize her time yet again. It was the 9:00pm drunken drama phone calls that took the on-call 24/7 to the hate her level.

Zandra suspected the inconsiderate bitch gave no thought to the fact that she herself had gone home at two this afternoon to prepare for the meet and greet function, leaving the lowly hired help to hold down the fort in her absence. Not to mention the useless kiss-ass newbie, whom they thought only got hired on the grounds that he had a dick. Maybe the old blackhead thought she could get something from that. Bmhahaha. Yeah right, good luck with that one. She obviously didn't have her gaydar on that day, or any day since he started three weeks ago. The man was an incompetent imbecile.

JT thought that in itself, was hilarious. As a petite, blonde, pocket rocket with a smart wit to match, her hour-glass figure and ample assets, she had a habit for drawing the boss' eye, and had even taken some of them up on the extra work curriculum. However, she had said straight up at the end of her first day a few years ago, "That is one boss I will never do."

She ventured up to the valet parking at the entrance to the venue, checking her lipstick in the rear vision mirror, before handing her keys over to the young attendant. He handed her the stub of a ticket in exchange and proceeded to park her car.

As she entered through the front door, she let out a sigh, whispering to herself, "And the fun begins," shaking her head while watching her boss pace back and forth at the entrance to the function room. She was feeling like she seriously could do with a pep talk from a tall dark scotch and coke, hold the ice. "Hell, forget the coke!" Before she could put that thought into motion, her boss turned and spied her out the corner of her eye. Wow! Even better, Anne's bloodshot eyes indicated she'd started the wine tasting hours ago by the look of it. When was that woman going to realize, she made an even bigger ass out of herself, after one glass, let alone the three bottles she looked like she'd crawled out of in preparation for tonight?

JT came up from behind and said over Zandra's shoulder, "Don't leave me alone with her, and I won't leave you alone with her. We pee together. Don't suppose we have time to sneak off to the general bar for a little reinforcement? The bitch looks like she has a head start on us all." The look on JT's face was priceless. Moving to stand side by side, Zandra and JT presented for duty as a united front. "Tempting, but the wicked bitch has already caught site of me. Give her three seconds and she'll start her screeching."

JT laughed, "If she drowns in the hand basin on a toilet break, just remember, you were with me when it happened, and we were nowhere near her at the time. Got it?" Zandra gave a sly sideways look and a smirking nod.

After the first week Zandra and JT had worked together, they had agreed that although Anne, may have intelligence, she was extremely lacking in the people skills department, resulting in their boss appearing quite crass. You could tell from her walking back into the office after doing a site safety induction for a new client that ripping her bra off and throwing it on the desk was deemed as being professional in her eyes. They also agreed that the woman was afraid of success, all too happy to put her finger in the pie as long as she wasn't the one who had to chase down the ingredients, make and bake it. She would insist that you supplied the plates and spoons to serve it up, while cackling, "Yes, yes it's my recipe. This is one I just whipped up." Once everything had been prepared for the client, she then signed on the dotted line and claimed it as another of her successful ventures. Then, behind the client's back, throwing it back on either Zandra or JT's desk for them to follow up on and find the client's requirements. At least Zandra and JT brought professionalism to the playground.

Zandra said to JT, "We really need to buy that winning lottery ticket."

JT replied, "Hey it's not like we haven't got a ticket. I want to know who I have to sleep with to get our numbers to come up.

Just keep in mind if it's a man, I'm not doing it."

Zandra looked at her in disbelief, "Not even for twenty million? Really? I have no idea how you managed to end up with a daughter."

JT scrunched her face up, "Okay so there was that one time, after which I can safely say, men have all that hair going on in places there shouldn't be hair, no hair where there should be, and, they all have that winkle thing happening." She then proceeded to make a gag motion to support the evidence she had presented. Gesturing up and down her body, JT smiled, "One hundred percent cuni-lingual fluent lesbian."

Zandra laughed while making her way into the room set-up for the night's function. Invitations had been sent out to about sixty companies and businesses. Fifty percent would be current clients and fifty percent would be new clients. The evening was based on feedback and promotion from new and current clients on how great the company's services were. It was also to drum up further contacts between both parties to better their own supply and demands. Even if, out of the prospective clients they only landed business from half of them, it would make for a successful night.

They encountered the queen B, in her most floral slur, "Where the fuck have you two been? When I give you something to do, I expect it to be done when I say."

JT's brows drew together in confusion, "What have we missed? I'm sorry Anne, but I'm not a mind reader. Everything has been prepared and organized in accordance with your demands, so again I ask, what did we miss or blatantly forget?" JT was never one to mince her words around Anne. She wasn't the doormat type, unless she was pulling it out from under Anne's feet, to then bitch-slap her with it.

Anne swayed slightly, "Never mind, I'll just have to do it myself. Honestly I have to do everything myself. This company couldn't run without me if I wasn't there to take care of every detail."

JT nodded, "While you're doing that then, I'm going to the toilet to freshen up."

Zandra followed, "I'll walk with you. One less thing to take care of once the guests arrive."

Once out of earshot they looked at one another and echoed in unison, "Bitch!"

Zandra told JT, "You know she rang me while I was driving here tonight demanding to know where I'd been? And then did a rant and rave about last-minute changes."

JT explained that she'd received a similar call, as they checked their appearances and snapped a photo against the wall, before taking their places at the door to receive and introduce various company directors. Rolling her eyes, Zandra wondered how long it would be before Anne let loose with that annoying cackle of hers.

Clients came and went, most avoiding Anne's drunken bragging, about how she was the leading recruitment agency, and how she could bend over backwards and kiss her own ass. She didn't believe in sharing the credit where it was due. No, as far as she was concerned, all her staff were overpaid and under worked. She liked to make out like she paid well above the award rate, a comical three cents an hour. She neglected to mention that her staff were frequently woken at all hours of the day and night with her staffing demands. The damn women was a fifty-five-year old insomniac, and if she didn't sleep, then nobody slept. Which would not be so bad except the pay packet did not reflect the twenty-four-hour a day, seven days a week phone calls. Not to mention no overtime or call-out bonuses. It simply covered the bills, with minimal left over for icing on top. At least now that her car was paid off, she could afford to pamper herself or have a rainy day occasionally.

Many clients made a point of approaching JT and Zandra, acknowledging their teamwork in supplying their staffing requirements. Two thirds of the prospective clients had handed out business cards with requests for contact in the near future, to sort out the numbers and areas of staffing required to cover increases in production or new positions opening up. By eleven o'clock the function was done and dusted, only leaving one drunk as a skunk Anne to put in a taxi and send on home. JT sighed, "Guess she didn't drown in the hand basin. Too bad we won't need that alibi tonight."

Zandra laughed, "The night is still early. Let's throw her head first in a cab and cut loose. I don't know about you, but I'm exhausted." JT thought it was a great plan. After helping their toxic boss into the back of a taxi cab and informing the driver, "Destination, Oz," the driver replied, with a thick Indian accent, "I do not know where that be mam." JT wrote it down for him and said, "Wow, what a great sense of humor you have. That's her address. Just make sure she gets home safe, payroll is Monday and we need her alive till then."

Turning to the valet they presented their collection tickets and waited.

JT gave Zandra a hug and a kiss on the cheek, and as her car approached first she said, "See you Monday. Have a good weekend."

Zandra waved, "You too. Try to stay out of trouble, and if you can't, then be safe."

While waiting for her car, all she could think about was getting home and soaking in a long hot bath and then sliding into the fresh sheets on her king size bed.

She stepped into her car and as the valet closed the door, she thanked him. She adjusted the seat and fastened her seatbelt. Thank God her apartment was only a short distance. She pulled out of the venue's driveway, noting that for a Friday night, there was a reasonable amount of traffic on the road.

As she approached the intersection, the lights turned green. Taking her foot off the brake, she placed it back on the accelerator to enter the intersection, just as a car ran the red light, ploughing into the driver's side of her vehicle. It happened so fast, everything just went black.

Slowly, she became aware of excruciating pain. It was too difficult to figure out where it originated from, her entire body hurt. Unable to do anything but moan, the paramedic said, "Stay still, do not move. You have been in an accident and we are waiting for the rescue team to arrive to get you out." Everything receded into that blackness where she didn't seem to be in any pain.

Emergency lights were flashing all around as police quickly had the area secured. Two ambulances were on scene, fire and rescue all arriving together at one on the most horrific scenes some of the emergency crews had ever laid eyes on. The police placed a blue tarp over a young, male passenger not wearing a seatbelt in the front of the offending vehicle. Two teams of paramedics were working frantically on the trapped drivers of both vehicles. Rescue teams were working around the paramedics to cut away the bent and twisted remains of the imploded vehicles. Paramedics were trying to stabilise their breathing and support the unconscious bodies.

Rescue teams worked as fast as possible to cut through the metal. "On the count of three, we lift the lid off this tin can," said senior rescue officer Harrison. "Then we can remove the door and give you full access."

Once the door was off, the paramedics swooped in with the aid of the rescue team. They managed to get Zandra on a spinal board and fit her with a neck brace. She was lifted onto a stretcher and locked into place in the back of the ambulance. Cutting clothes and attaching monitors, administering an IV, they were doing all they could to stabilise her as the ambulance raced to the nearest hospital, sirens blaring and lights flashing with a police escort.

CHAPTER 2

Destiny was tired - it had been a long day. When he thought about it, it had been a longer week and even longer year. He was exhausted though it wasn't like he could take time off. He couldn't even remember what it was like not to have the responsibilities of all mankind trapping him in this place. He'd long ago given up hope of ever being free of his prison. Shaking his head, he thought of all those worthless, sick and twisted people who got less for murder. They knew they would either die from an attack in prison or get parole. It was a win, win situation.

There was no such thing as parole where he was standing or in this instance sitting.

He turned the page of the volume named Joseph Henry, the newborn baby who had just taken his first breath and opened his blurry eyes to the bright lights surrounding him. He was placed in the arms of a loving mother who would distract him from all the strange noises that were suddenly so loud.

Destiny sighed at the unmistakable smell of ink blanching paper. He blew a breath of warm air to set the ink, waited a minute for it to dry, then closed the book and placed it on the shelf with the knowledge that this was now a closed volume. The boy's destiny had just been sealed. He would now be passed onto his brother to take care of. He would not touch the volume again until it was archived on the day of Joseph Henry's death. The only thing he could tell of a life span was by the bulk of the volume. Joseph Henry would probably be near fifty when his life force would cease to exist.

Death would have his name appear

with a date, time and location for collection. His brother had already collected the volumes for today's collections.

He often wondered why he held the realm of Destiny. His mother always explained it was because as the eldest of her immortal children, he had been born blind and that all mankind's destiny must be equal in its prescription.

He felt a stir of air and a shift in his surroundings. Something was different. There was a presence unlike when one of his kin came to visit. He moved back through the many shelves of the library toward the sitting area where his desk was located. As he progressed, the foreign sensation grew stronger. As the bookshelves opened up into the main room, he could hear the soft sounds of breathing and the smell of rose geranium, not unlike those from his mother's garden, yet he knew it was not his mother's essence that filled the room. It was different. He also knew it was not that of his sisters, Karma or Delirium. It was definitely not an Immortal. The person did not have the power that would emanate from a God.

As he stepped towards the three seater sofa, he held his hand out in front of himself to better feel the shift in energy. His hand touched the heel of a shoe. Following along the couch, there was a soft-skinned foot inside the shoe, an ankle that wasn't skinny and bony but also not heavy- set, but structurally sound. His hand worked further up the solid calf, knee and thigh. Voluptuous, was the only word that came to mind, his brain trying to understand exactly what the intruder was doing in his space.

She did not appear to be moving apart from the inhale and exhale of shallow breaths. He returned to his desk to consider the situation. Maybe if he left her alone for a while, she would simply return to wherever she came from. The air became chilled as his brother entered the room, "Hey brother of mine, what's the skinny?"

Destiny replied, "I don't have a clue.

Maybe you can tell me. I didn't think she was a skinny female though."

Death took on a puzzled look, "What in hell are you going on about? I'm not following."

Destiny raised his hand and pointed in the general direction of the couch, without saying a word to indicate his discomfort. Death glanced over his shoulder, his head snapping back in the direction of his brother, "Damn it! Shit! What have you done? Who is she?"

Destiny grew angry with the implied words, "I have no idea who she is, how she got here or even where she came from. I felt a change in the room and next thing you know, I'm finding her on my couch." His voice became more intense with every word." I didn't bring her here, and I don't recall ordering home delivery from the Crisco Catalogue."

"Well do you think we should wake her up? It would be a start to finding out those questions you don't have answers for. You know I can't touch her or she will become my problem, and seeing as I'm not missing anyone on my roll call, that makes you batter up."

"Before I do this, can you give me something to work with? What does she look like? How old would you say she is? Any notable features that we could use to identify where she may come from?" It was the first time Destiny had ever envied his brother's ability to see. He wanted to know what the feel of her skin under his hands had looked like.

Death took in her appearance, "She has hair the colour you live in, she seems to be wearing a party dress of some description, and she looks to be late twenty something. She has a voluptuous curve to her body in all the right places. No visible birthmarks or tattoos, but then her body is covered. She seems to be in a state of stasis, breathing, but not moving. Hhmm my best guess is to call Walt Disney, Snow White has been found," laughing to himself, "Maybe you should kiss her, Prince of Destiny."

Sometimes Destiny really disliked his siblings. He knew they all took their duties with dedication and devotion, but honestly, they had a fucked up sense of humour when it came to their sibling's shortcomings.

Death's ill-timed attempt at a joke aggravated his anger. "Very Funny. Ha-ha!" Sarcasm dripping, "I think it's time you left if you aren't going to be of any significant help." He did not like to admit he resented his brother's eyes being able to see what he could not.

He had also noted the underlying appreciation in his brother's voice as he ogled the female on his couch, and he had no intentions of turning this situation into a territorial pissing contest with him. He moved to stand between Death and the female, in case he suddenly thought to touch her and remove her from his domain.

He didn't understand why he was standing his ground, in that he had never been possessive by nature. Death took a sidestep around Destiny, his hand rising, reaching. Destiny's arm shot out to latch onto his brother's wrist. At the contact, he saw a mental image of what his brother's eyes were focused on. His sharp intake of breath left him speechless. He could hear a growling noise as if from a distance getting closer as it intensified.

Still holding his brother's wrist, his mind's vision turned to his sightless face, carrying an animalistic snarl. He realised then that the noise was coming from his own throat. Quickly gathering himself, he could only manage one word, "Don't!"

He released his brother's wrist with such force that Death was thrown across the room. Mid throw, Death vanished and reappeared near his brother. "Dude! What the fuck?" Destiny simply replied, "Just don't."

Death sighed, "Whatever. I got places to be people to see. You know how to reach me." And with that he disappeared.

Destiny locked his realm down tight. Nobody was coming in or going out without him knowing, his family would have to announce themselves before arriving. At the moment, he had all the visitors he could deal with and he needed to think. He paced back and forth trying to find a way to establish who she was.

He placed his hand on her shoulder, bracing himself, ready to be assaulted by a fast forward flash of the female's memories, but there was nothing, just dark space. She wasn't even in the midst of a dream. It was like she didn't exist prior to magically appearing on his couch. There was nothing, just emptiness.

He sat back on his heels, chin resting between his fingers and thumb. In her present state she would be more than safe on the couch, while he took care of his base needs, a long, hot shower to ease the pounding in his head. He felt drained and more than a little confused.

He moved into his bedroom, grabbed a change of clothes, threw them on the bed and entered his private bathroom. He had the luxury of simply making things happen with his mind, he didn't have to shave with a razor, he just willed the facial hair to be gone. He didn't have to do washing, he just willed his clothes to be gone, and new ones were willed to fill his drawers. He didn't care what they looked like, he went for the feel of the fabric on his skin and the comfort of them. He definitely did not do wool, it made his skin itch. He didn't have to worry about colours as he only wore black. Black was the only colour he felt an affinity with as it was the colour he knew best, he lived in blackness. All luxuries aside, he loved a good, hot shower to ease tired muscles, aches and pains. It also gave him pause to think.

CHAPTER 3

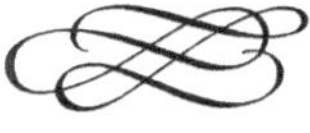

She slowly started to stir. It was like being caught in the undercurrent after being taken down by a wave at the beach. As she tried to grasp onto her consciousness, it would pull her back, disorienting her again, and unable to work out which way was up. She took a couple of deep breaths before opening her eyes, to stave off the nausea. "Okay, don't rush it. Must have hit my head." She tried to remember what she'd been doing, but there was nothing. It was like the cupboard inside her head was bare. Opening her eyes slowly, she glanced around. Nothing looked familiar, not the room, nor the couch she seemed to be on. She carefully lifted to a sitting position, her head hurt, and her vision swam. She sat for a moment collecting her strength to stand.

"I either drank way too much, or I hit my head pretty hard. These shoes are not worth further damage," she said, kicking off her shoes, she thought, "That's a start in the right direction," and things were looking-up, she still had clothes on.

She had no idea where she was, there was nobody around to be seen. She thought that maybe, if she looked around some, things might come back to her. All she needed was something familiar to focus on and hopefully it would jog her memory.

She saw an uncluttered desk, heavy set, hand-carved and with a masculine sense to it. After a quick glance she established that no answers would be found here. Moving on, she glanced at the closest bookshelf in what looked to be an immense library. She noticed the odd similarity of all the books on the shelf resembled each other, all bar the different names along the spine, along with a code. No, wait, they were dates. "How bizarre," she whispered to herself. Still, nothing was leaping out at her to put the pieces together.

She noticed a door that let out of the room and figured in for a penny, in for a pound. She exited the room cautiously, but, nope still nothing and nobody in sight. To go to the left or to the right? Eeny, meany, miny, moe. Okay awkward. What was she, five? She turned to the right and proceeded to walk the distance to the first door which was slightly ajar. Senses on high alert, she gently pushed the door open enough that she could see a large king size bed in the middle of an enormous bedroom. She approached the bed to see clothes on it. Black sweats definitely not her size. Okay, alrighty then, she turned to make her exit as the door to what resembled a private bathroom opened. She held her breath.

From out of the mist escaping the bathroom stepped a man, huge and towering, at least six foot four, with hair as black as night. He had a towel wrapped round his hips, riding low. His arms were thick as tree trunks. With the body of a Greek Adonis, not an ounce of fat anywhere, he was pure muscle. Her eyes widened as he started to move toward her. "Oh crap." was all she could think at that moment, which left her with the impression that he was an unknown factor. She was certain that she would remember all of him. If she had played with all that man had going on, she was one hundred and ten percent sure, without a doubt, it would be scorched into her brain's hard drive. As he came closer, she realized that he almost looked right through her, as if she were not standing in front of him at all.

Okay, she had seen some weird shit in her lifetime, but she was not about to have him walk through her as though she was invisible. She carefully lifted her foot to take a step sideways to avoid collision. She had only just transferred her weight when his hand grabbed her arm. She tried to pull free from his hold. He wasn't hurting her, but she felt uncomfortable after thinking herself unnoticed.

His face turned to her, and she looked up into the blackest eyes she had ever seen, so black it was hard to tell, but it looked as if the irises had been swallowed whole by the pupil. Oh my God! She was stunned when she realized he really couldn't see her for real, he was blind.

Trying not to hyperventilate, she asked, "Who are you? Where am I? Nothing looks familiar. Why does my head hurt like I've spent the entire weekend bar hopping every airport from Australia to Vegas?" Okay, she was starting to sound crazy and unstable. There had to be a logical explanation for her current dilemma if only she could remember.

He still had hold of her arm, and he never did like looking into his own sightless eyes, so he dropped his hand, breaking the connection and allowing him to focus on the female and what she was saying. He heard the panic in her voice that left him feeling uncomfortable, in a strange way he did not understand. He knew that if he was going to figure out the events that led her to his realm then he needed her calm and collected. "Breathe female, slowly." His voice was deep and commanding.

She felt her legs weaken and realized she had been close to passing out from hyperventilation. She staggered the couple of steps to the king size bed and sat down, placing her head between her knees. After a couple of shaky breaths she sat back up, head still harping like a bitch.

He could hear her settling into a regular breathing pattern. He then recalled her saying something amid her rabble about being in pain. He moved closer, placing his hands in her hair and his body tensed as his fingers came into contact with hair as fine as silk. He could imagine the feel of it brushing on his chest, moving down his body. Just then his mind's vision cleared to see that from where she sat, she was level with his waist and that she was currently eyeing his muscle definition. He focused his attention on the tempo of the pain in her head, closing his useless eyes. He felt the tentacles like electric cables following them back to the source and like flicking a switch, he tamped it down like a volume dial on a stereo.

Finally her head had become bearable, and she breathed a sigh as she no longer felt nauseous. The stranger's hands were still buried in her hair as she tilted her head up, taking in all that smooth hard skin, till she reached his face and eyes. He swiftly broke the connection, reaching down for his sweats and slid them out from under her, where she had sat on the bed.

"Thank you," she said in a half whisper. She didn't care how he did it. All she knew was his touch had taken her pain away.

She summoned the strength to ask him, "Who are you? How did you do that? Where am I? What am I doing here?" She was firing off questions too quick for him to answer, and if she kept it up, she was going to become hysterical again.

He waited for her to take a breath and grabbed the first chance to speak, "This is my home, in the realm of Destiny," he raised his thumb to point at his chest as a

dominant male would to indicate owner-
ship or possession. She smirked to herself,
'Neanderthal'.

"Okay, well I'm sure there must be a
reasonable explanation for you bringing
me here. Wait, what? I've never heard of
the place, where exactly am I?" She was
even more confused now from his
statement.

"You're sitting on my bed, in my bedroom, in my house, in my realm." Oh he
did not just roll his eyes at her and speak
to her like she was three that just pissed
her off.

Everything was just getting stranger
and weirder by the minute. The big guy
turned to step back towards the bathroom
with his sweats over one shoulder. She
lifted her right arm, and reaching across
her chest, she pinched her left arm, "Ouch!
Well there goes my dream theory."

The big guy returned, wearing his
black sweats with no shirt, showing off his
muscular body. He had a physique the
ladies would admire. Hell knew she
couldn't take her eyes off him. "Are you

hungry?" he asked, as a growl of lion ran round her stomach, making her aware that she was a tad on the peckish side and had no idea when she last ate.

"Yeah, I could do with bite to eat," she said, thinking she could really sink her teeth into a side of his ribs. "I am hungry," she replied, smirking to herself.

"Well if you would like to freshen up, I'll get started on organizing something to eat." He gestured to his bathroom, "You will find fresh towels on the rack." Then he was gone, out the door as fast as his feet could carry him.

She moved toward the bathroom. Once inside, she could see a spacious area containing a toilet, a large bath, basin and a shower that looked like it could fit a small gathering. Okay so the big guy would take up a considerable amount of space in there. She closed the door and locked it. She glanced in the mirror that covered the entire wall behind the basin. She looked as if she'd been pulled through a hedge backwards kicking and screaming. Stepping out of her dress and underwear, she

turned and opened the shower door, getting in.

Turning on the hot water she arranged
the taps and moved under the spray.
Tilting her head back, she borrowed the
big guy's shampoo and conditioner. Then
using his body-wash, with the expensive
fragrant gel, she soaped up her skin. She
could feel the tension of all the unan-
swered questions washing down the drain.
She would get some answers while she ate.

After towelling herself dry, she
wrapped herself in her towel and entered
the bedroom. Looking around, her eyes
stopped at the dresser and unrepentantly
approaching it, she acquired a shirt. She
almost felt petite, it was long enough to
reach just above her knee, and she had to
cuff the sleeves. Placing the towel in the
hamper, she made her way out of the bathroom through the bedroom and into the
hall. She listened for any indication of
where to locate the kitchen, feeling lost in
the unfamiliar surroundings.

CHAPTER 4

After leaving the female to get comfortable, Destiny walked down the hall to the kitchen. There he found himself lost as to what she might be interested in eating. It felt odd for him to want to please someone other than himself. He opted for some scrambled eggs with a side of toast. He served it up, placed a coffee cup and a glass on the bench and walked down the hall toward the bedroom. He found her standing in the hall just outside the bedroom. "I was trying to figure out which direction the kitchen was in," she said as he approached.

He abruptly stopped, waited, and then

held his hand out to offer guidance. She glanced at his hand for only a second before placing hers inside his. It was warm and smooth and the connection felt right. She like the way it radiated a warm tingle rushing throughout her body, like static electricity, her body awakening to the touch of a lover.

His mind's eye focused and saw what she was looking at with her hand inside his. Before she could look up at him, he said, "Close your eyes. I can't focus on my bearings when you look at me like that." More confused than ever, she did as he asked.

She allowed him to lead her into the kitchen, where he promptly dropped her hand. She felt the loss, and found herself thinking if that's what one hand on her could do then she could only imagine what him touching her elsewhere would be like, addictive most likely. In a gruff voice he told her, "You can open your eyes. Have a seat. I didn't know what you would eat, so I just went with eggs. Would you like tea, coffee or juice?"

"Coffee would be great."

He moved to the bench on the other side of the kitchen, "How do you have it?"

"White with one sugar, thanks." She sat down on a stool and took a bite of her eggs. Damn, either she was starving, or these eggs were really good. She had wolfed half of them down when he returned, placing her coffee on the bench.

He let out a disgruntled sigh, "Okay, we need to talk." He folded his arms and leaned back against the corner of the bench, "I need to know your name first of all."

She paused with the coffee cup halfway to her mouth, "I, um, my name is…" A long pause, 'Okay what is my name?' Her brows drew together, 'Why can't I remember who I am?' She tried again saying out loud in a less than confident manner, "My name is… "Still nothing, frustration formed tears in her eyes that she was not going to let loose. 'Suck it up you're stronger than that.' "I can't tell you what I don't know. When I woke on that couch in the other room, I felt like I had been on a long weekend bender and I was hung over. Did you mickey my drink or something, is that how I got here?" She looked at the food and coffee he had served her and suddenly felt nervous although that nervousness was quickly suppressed by her overriding anger.

She stood up from her stool, stalked around the bench and proceeded to poke the big guy in the chest while demanding, "What did you do to me? Did you drug me before bringing me back to your place? Did you think I would just play along with your sick twisted fantasies?" She had gone from pointed finger to both fists pounding on his chest.

He moved so fast she couldn't block his intentions. He grabbed both her wrists and fastened them behind her where she could no longer reach him. She struggled to free herself, closed her eyes, tilted her head back and head butted his chest.

Lucky, if her head had hit on target she would have busted his nose, the little devil. All patience gone, he tightened his grip, bent down next to her ear and whispered,

"If you don't stop this absurd behavior right this second I will put you over my knee and spank you."

"Fuck you, pervert," she replied through heavy breathing that she would not admit came from anything more than her struggle to free herself. It had nothing to do with the strong arms wrapped around her, the smell of his closeness or the fact that he wasn't wearing a shirt.

He bent one knee toward the floor and she was being lifted over his shoulder. She was mortified, she wasn't wearing panties, and what the hell was he, a caveman? She bounced against his shoulder as he stormed out of the room and was striding down the hall and into the room with the couch she had woken up in. He placed her down on it, took a couple of steps back and proceeded to pace back and forth. He ran one hand through his hair. "Okay, I want you to sit there, shut up and listen. I'm only going to go over this once. If you have questions, you can ask when it's your turn to swap info. It's the only way I can put the pieces together. Do you understand?"

"Sure. I can work with that." She thought he had a valid point, and possibly some answers.

He began "My name is Destiny. I am the eldest son of the Goddess Cosmo. I have been around since man first walked the earth. I took on my duties as of my twenty-first cycle, whereby my mother handed off her duties to me. Likewise, my brothers and sisters were handed their delegated duties at their twenty-first cycle. I determine what a person's life will be bestowed with and what lessons a person may have to learn before they return to the fold. The books on these shelves are all current lives being lived out. Once their life is sealed, they are filed on the shelf and they are then collected from the shelves on the date they will take their last breath and their life force ceases to exist as they know it. They are then no longer my responsibility." He paused, "I was born blind, however some part of my mind can see through the connection of touch. I can visualize in my mind, seeing through the eyes of the person being touched. I see what they see. I have no idea who you are, or where you came from. I most certainly did not bring you here and I have not figured out how to send you back."

Okay she didn't like the sound of that last bit, it made her feel as if she was a burden, like he couldn't wait to unload her.

"I was performing my duties in here and I found you on the couch. My brother entered the room shortly after and we had words regarding you. He left, and I locked my realm up so that nobody could come or go. That's the sum of it. Any questions?"

"So that was the reason you told me to close my eyes in the hall, to stop you from seeing what I was looking at?"

"Yes, it disoriented me."

"Guess you don't redecorate very often," she commented. Could she be that evil to move stuff around when he pissed her off?

"No, and I'd like it kept that way," he said sarcastically, almost as if he could hear her thoughts. She poked her tongue at him and then felt like a brat for doing so.

She questioned, "So you're saying that I came from nowhere and that I was unconscious, for how long?"

"Maybe an hour, I'm not really sure," he shrugged. "The only thing I can think of, is to give out the call to my family, one at a time, and see if they know of you. I will stay in contact with you so that I can see through your eyes, but do not touch them, do you understand?"

"Yeah, is that because it would mess with your vision?"

"No, it means they can take you from my dimension. I don't have the ability to navigate anyone else's realms. If they take you from here, I may not be able to find you."

"So when you use my eyes to see, does that mean you can hear my thoughts too?" She needed to know to keep her thoughts in check if that was the case.

"No, just what your eyes see, I can't hear your thoughts," although the idea made him curious, and he grinned slyly.

He hated to admit it, but the interaction with this female was actually enjoyable. He found her challenging and somewhat entertaining. It made for a nice change from his usual existence.

"I can't keep referring to you as female. As long as you are here I will call you by what you are, 'Enigma,' a puzzle to be solved. I feel that's suitable, any complaints?" He raised an eyebrow.

"No? Good. I've had enough for today, I need sleep. I'll notify my brother I need to speak with him." He started to leave the room.

"Hey, forgetful much?" She placed her hands on her hips.

CHAPTER 5

"Follow me, I only have my bed. I don't have sleep overs and I can protect you better." That was his argument, and he was sticking to it.

"Okay, but if you're immortal, then why do you need sleep and how can you tell what time it is, day or night?" She thought this was odd.

"We all need to conserve and realign our energy. If we didn't, we would go insane, our realms would implode and we would be segregated, unable to continue our assigned duties." She followed while listening. "The time of day or night is irrelevant to me. I sleep when my body is tired, and at the moment I'm exhausted. How long I sleep is unpredictable, it could be an hour or it could be several. However my days and nights are believed to mimic those of your Southern Hemisphere. Sometimes I may not sleep for days at a time."

As she unceremoniously got into his king sized bed and laid her head on the pillow with a yawn, she wondered what time it really was. She hadn't seen a clock anywhere throughout the place. Her eyelids grew heavy as Destiny climbed in next to her. He took up a lot of space in the king size bed but still managed to keep his distance. Destiny lay there listening to her breathe. Her breathing changed to slow and deep. After a while the sound became soothing and his eyes closed and he gave himself up to the numbness of sleep.

Something strange slowly disturbed his slumber. It was warm and full of soft curves. In his sleep, he had wrapped around all that softness like it was his next breath. He'd never taken a female to his bed, though he'd imagined it, and he'd used his brother Morpheus's sand to dream of it. Not wanting to tempt himself or lose control, he tried to move away. She followed, snuggling in closer, wriggling against his cock that was fast beginning to throb from being nuzzled. He ground his teeth. Just what he needed more complications. Touch was not something he needed at the moment either.

He turned to his back and tried to think about other stuff when she rolled over and cuddled up to him placing a hand on his bare stomach. That was his undoing. He slid his hand silently down to where the hand on his stomach rested. He laid his hand over hers. Her hand was so soft and so small compared to his. He wanted to know what it would feel like wrapped around his cock. That wasn't all. He wanted to know what her smart little mouth on him would feel like as he ran his hands through her hair. What he wouldn't give to see and feel it at the same time. Now he was so hard it was painful, he needed relief but couldn't take care of it in this position. His breathing heavy, he was about to get up, when he felt her move.

She rolled over. The very second her body left his he realized how isolated and alone his realm really was. He wanted her to stay with him, he didn't want her to leave. In the treacherous aftermath of his body's awakening, he rose from the bed and stormed toward the shower.

She awoke to the sound of someone moaning in pain. As she became familiar with her surroundings, she climbed across the bed. She rushed to the open door of the bathroom and froze. All thought left her as her knees grew weak at the sight of a very naked, very aroused Destiny.

His eyes were closed, his lips slightly parted, the water was trailing down his body making her thirsty. His hand was circling his cock, slowly stroking it. The head appeared on the upward stroke. She licked her lips, breathing heavily, she wanted to touch him. She wanted to be in the shower with him. He opened his eyes and she let out a squeak, forgetting for a split second that he couldn't see her. He stopped his strokes, he'd heard her, she was sure of it.

He was sure he was no longer alone, he could sense he was being watched. At first he paused mid-stroke. The thought of her watching him pleasure himself only made him hotter. A part of him wanted to know what she would do. He leaned against the tiles and started moving his hand again. He slid his other hand down to roll his tight ball sack. He lightly drew them down, a moan slipping from his lips. He was nowhere near close to losing his load and his patience was slipping, more frustrated than ever.

She didn't know what part of her brain got damaged when she got here but before she could think much on it, she was lifting the hem of her shirt, sliding it up her body, and lifting it over her head. She silently opened the shower door, he would either welcome or reject her, but she was working on the basis that you only live once.

She closed the door behind her, placing a hand on his chest. This time it was his turn to freeze. A tremor ran through his body. He didn't say anything, just stood still, waiting. He was testing her, his hands dropped to his sides in tight fists, his control very near breaking point, as her hand was laid against his chest.

He didn't notice he had been holding his breath. He should stop this before it went any further. His guilt at not wanting to swiftly dispersed, leaving him without the ability to move away. Her forehead rested on his chest next to her hand. In his mind's eye, his vision cleared, and he found he was watching her hand trail down over his abs. She turned her knuckles to his skin as her hand slipped between his engorged penis and his pubis, her thumb circled the head. "Hell, have mercy," he growled through grinding teeth. Did she know she was setting him on fire? She must do, he was shaking. Did she realise he was watching through her eyes? It was the most erotic, sensual experience he had ever had.

Her restraint was barely there, not wanting his rejection, but her resolve finally snapped. She knew at this point there was no stopping this now. She eased her grip over his cock, he was so large her fingers couldn't meet. As she drew her hand down, running her thumb along the underside, he mumbled something. The blood pounding in her ears made it difficult to decipher. She slightly lifted her head, pressing kisses to his chest and then trailing the water rivulets down. She reached eye to eye with his weeping prick and her tongue came out to swipe leisurely over the crown. That was all he could take, he was broken, shattered, his hands diving into her hair. "I can't take much more of your teasing," he moaned as her hot, wet mouth enveloped his flesh. He was igniting and melting at the same time. He could see her hand around the base, as she withdrew to the crown, he could see his own heavily veined cock. She pulled him free, then pursed her lips and held his entry to a slow tight fit. She moaned as he hit the back of her throat, the vibrations setting him on edge. Winding him up tighter, she sensed his closeness. He'd swollen further in her mouth and he was as hard as steel.

She applied the flat of her tongue to the underside of the crown, added pressure from the roof of her mouth and started to pump. She felt the jerk of his cum moving up his shaft as she milked him, swallowing every spurt of his hot cum. "Fuuuuuck," he rode out his orgasm moving until his knees grew weak. He tugged on her hair to bring her up against his heaving chest, wrapped his arms around her and buried his face in her neck.

"What have I done?" he thought, "I've bound myself to this woman. I can't sustain another day without ever having this again."

CHAPTER 6

He wanted her bound to him to, he just wasn't sure where to start. He wanted her everything, but just didn't know how to get it. He began kissing her neck just under her right ear and then turned her back to the shower's tiled wall. He kissed and nipped his way along her jaw. "Close your eyes for me, I want to share my world with you. Just feel," he whispered against her lips. Then he was there, his lips gentle on hers, his tongue sliding along the seam asking for entry. She parted for him and his kiss grew deeper, more intense. Her tongue met his, dancing heatedly with passion for dominance. He drew away slowly, resting his forehead against hers, their breaths mingling heavily.

The fire ignited throughout her body making her ache. She wanted him, all of him. His hands, his mouth, and she needed him inside her. It was like she couldn't breathe if he stopped. "Don't stop, I need more," she begged.

He liked the sound of her pleas. He ran his arm around her waist, tilting slightly to take her nipple in his mouth. He flicked it with his tongue, then ran circles round it, the size of a ripe cherry. He could feel his need for her growing. He growled as he released her puckered nipple to focus on her neglected one. He slid his free hand down her side over her curvy hip, he liked the way her softness filled his hand.

She couldn't think with his mouth teasing her nipple like he was savouring a delicious dessert. His hand trailed down her side, sending shocks of tingling electricity through her body. Her clit was starting to throb, she was wanton and needy. "Please, Destiny," she whimpered.

Her legs felt like jelly and he was the only thing keeping her upright. Pausing from his assault on her over sensitive nipples, he ordered, "Open for me. Spread your legs. I've got you. Let yourself go."

No sooner had she complied, then she felt his finger along her wet folds as he cupped her. "Do you want this? I can stop now," he lied.

"Yes, please," she replied on a breathless hiss as his fingers parted her lips.

"You're dripping wet," he said as he dipped his middle finger inside. "Shhhh, just feel."

What was he talking about? All she could do was feel, but she needed more. He slipped a second finger inside, and curling his fingers, he started a slow ride.

She was climbing, still not enough, she was on the edge. He withdrew and found her swollen clit playing circles around it. Oh God, she needed both. She needed him stretching her pussy, filling it and the pressure on her clit.

He knew she couldn't take much more, so he let go of her waist and bent down lifting one leg over his shoulder, buried his fingers deep and sampled her clit with a swipe of his tongue. "Oh God, that's it," she threw her head back as he French kissed her nub. He sucked it between his lips and teased the exposed nerves, pumping her pussy with strong hard strokes. She saw sparks behind her eyelids, screaming at the top of her lungs. Her orgasm passed over her, under her and through her, it was like lightning, it scorched her to her soul. After fighting for air for several long minutes, breathing around the aftershocks, he released her. She started to slide down the wall, boneless. He stood, winding his arm around her to pull her in close. He placed a hand on her face. Running his thumb over her lips he kissed her gently, she could taste herself on his lips.

"Thank you," he said quietly.

"For what?" she giggled.

"For opening my eyes to new possibilities," he kissed her again gently.

It showed her a vulnerable side other than strength and dominance. It made her sad that she would be leaving when they worked out how to send her back. They got out of the shower, dried off in silence, and then wrapped their towels loosely around themselves.

"So what now? What's our next move in figuring out what's happening and why I'm here?" she asked. Not able to face him for his reply, she busied herself with her hair. He wound his arms around her as she watched him in the mirror.

He was unsure what to make of what was happening between them. He'd been a prisoner in his realm for such a long time. He'd known there was an entire world out there that he was an invaluable part of everyone's future. He got that, but he was starting to question at what expense. His brothers and sisters could walk amongst them. They got to play a hands on part in their duties. He only knew he was safe and secure within his realm. Would he give it all up for a chance with the woman pressed up against his chest?

Did she have someone looking for her? Was there someone waiting for her to return? Could he let her go? She had come to mean more than just a warm body, she was someone he could talk to and care for, protect. His chest ached at the thought of her leaving. Did she want to leave?

The vision in his mind cleared and he once again saw through her eyes, his arms around her waist. Then slowly she raised her eyes to the mirror above the sink. Her reflection and his, intertwined together, had him enthralled. He liked the sight of her like that. He watched himself kiss the side of her neck, her arm rising to rest her hand at the back of his skull. He saw the parting of her lips, the flush of her cheeks as her body became more pliant. Through her half-lidded eyes, he saw the towel fall away from her body, his hands cupping her breasts. She looked beautiful, the most perfect thing he'd ever seen. Her head tilted further to the side for better access. Her eyes closed, to better savor the sensations.

"Please, keep your eyes open. I want to see all of you when you cum for me this time." Not wanting to miss a single thing if this was to be their last time together. He wanted to remember every fragment forever and always.

She reopened her eyes wide with the waking realization that he could see her, she felt naked and exposed. She could do this for him and for herself knowing they would both remember this moment no matter where they were. It would be their parting gift.

He rolled her nipples making them harden and turn a dark pink. She licked her lips, her mouth gone dry. She placed both her hands flat on the bench either side of the basin. She watched his right-hand snake down slowly to her aching pussy. He parted her lips, running a finger through her wetness as he zeroed in on her throbbing nub. Her hips began a rhythmic sway of their own volition.

Seeing through her eyes, he loved the way her body reacted to his touch. He tilted her body with his left hand on her hip, then guided his thickened shaft to her entrance and in one hard flex he seated himself. She was tight, slick and hot, and he thought he would combust in that split second. He stilled, letting her grow accustomed to his size, and to regain his control. He was in between heaven and hell, her inner muscles contracting tightly around him, he couldn't stay still a moment longer. He started to move while he watched.

She was stretched. He reached a depth that had all her nerves surrounding him alive. Her muscles pulsed and contracted around him, adjusting to accommodate. She felt branded, owned. He started to glide almost all the way out, paused then pushed all the way in, the head of his cock bumping the mouth of her cervix. She arched her back to give him better access. As his passion grew, so did his tempo, moving harder and faster. He worked circles round her nub, grinding her with steady stokes, they were both breathing hard. He asked her to touch herself, holding the front of her shoulder for anchorage, pumping deeper and harder while watching as her fingers danced around and over her clit. He could feel her orgasm squeezing his cock, milking him, taking his breath away.

Her orgasm had hit so hard she was seeing stars from the contractions of gripping him like a vice. She felt his hot seed filling her as a deep satisfaction swept over them. It was like they were one.

He slid from her warmth and lifted her in his arms. He took her to his bed. He kissed her, then intertwined, they fell asleep.

CHAPTER 7

Zandra's eyelids felt heavy, they didn't want to open. They felt like they were swollen shut. Her head was pounding and everything sounded so loud. There was a beeping noise worse than a persistent bird outside your bedroom window when trying to sleep in on Sunday morning. "Annie, get your gun that noise has to stop," she slurred incoherently.

She heard the scraping of a chair on linoleum and tried to turn her head. Damn that was not a smart idea. It was the throttle for the jack-hammer that was currently cracking her skull in two like a coconut, and it had just gone from zero to sixty in three seconds.

There was a soft dinging noise drowned out by the buzz in her head. Her arm was lifted, and it felt like someone was inflating a floatie. She wasn't going swimming. It was too cold to go in the water. She started to fight until she heard the voice of a woman in a calming tone. "Miss Wilson, Zandra, you were in an accident. You need to calm down. You're going to be alright." The woman's voice was joined by another, "I'll page Doctor Fischer." Then she was alone with women number one. Obviously she had worked out she was in no way fit to be swimming either. She'd removed the floatation device from her arm, well that was a relief.

"Miss Wilson, can you hear me? Try not to move until the doctor has seen you," she continued, "My name is Sarah. I am one of the nurses that work here."

Here? Where was here? How did I get here? What happened? Why couldn't she open her eyes, and who was holding her down? He body felt weighted, like the neighbour's cat and dog had curled up on her bed and were using her body as a pillow.

"Welcome back Miss Wilson, I'm Doctor Fischer," a deep voice said from the bottom of the bed. "Not to distress you, but you had us all quite worried over the last few days. You sustained considerable injuries from your accident," he continued, "We just need to run some basic tests and then we can look at making you comfortable."

He proceeded to poke and prod her in places that were raw. It was like he knew all her vulnerable sore spots, of which there seemed to be many. She thought this was his sick twist on playing Marco-Polo, she still couldn't open her eyes. Maybe that was a good thing at the moment, she couldn't see how badly hurt her body was. She couldn't remember the accident, what accident? Her head was still throbbing, and she was finding it hard to focus on all the stuff happening around her.

Dazed and confused, she felt someone softly lift her head, the sound of tape being released, and the rubber band wrapped around her head started to tighten in her temples. "We are just going to remove some of the bandages, due to intra-cranial swelling. We covered your eyes in case the optic nerves were affected. You may find that with the residual swelling, it alters your vision and objects may not appear as normal. You may not be able to see clearly. You need to be prepared that your vision may be affected to the extreme where you won't be able to focus at all."

"Doctor, I get what you're saying, but at the moment my head is taking up concentration. Can you stop it from throbbing like a bitch? Maybe then I can worry about whether I can see or not."

The doctor replied in a generic non-committal bedside tone, "Of course Miss Wilson." There were some whispers between the nurse called Sarah and Doctor what's his name. Sarah left the room, returning shortly after to inform her that she was going to give her something for the pain. Sarah said, "You may feel sleepy, but the pain should start to fade soon."

There was warmth that filled her and within a short while she felt tipsy. 'That was some hair of the dog,' she thought. The doctor resumed removing the bandages, "Can we dim the lights please nurse?" he requested as he lifted the cotton patches gently, "Okay, now Zandra I want you to slowly try to open your eyes."

Her eyelids felt like they were glued shut and her eyeballs were hard-boiled eggs. She managed to crack them open. She must look like she'd been in a bad pub brawl. The bruising around her eyes stung like a swarm of bees had attacked her, and the room was black.

"Zandra I'm just going to have a quick look at your eyes," he took a small penlight out of his pocket. Flicking it on, he waved it quickly in the corner of her left eye, then her right. "As your pupils are non-responsive, I suspect that there is still residual swelling placing pressure on the optic nerves. As that swelling recedes, your vision should slowly return. At the moment however, we need to replace the bandages to prevent any possible damage. We will try again tomorrow and see if there is any change. Nurse would you see that Miss Wilson has fresh dressings before the lights are turned back on?" Before he could escape, Zandra asked, "Doctor, how long will it take for me to see again?"

Sighing, the doctor chose his words carefully, "I wish I could give you an answer, but in cases like this, everyone is different. You just have to take it one day at a time. Try not to worry, stress is something that will only slow your recovery down." He proceeded to have hushed words with the nurse before saying, "I've given the nurse some instructions in hope we can make you more comfortable, and I will call on you tomorrow to check your progress."

Nurse Sarah washed her hands, applied sterile gloves, and approached the bed. As she redressed Zandra's eyes with patches and dressings she explained, "Doctor Fischer has instructed me to make you comfortable. Would you like some ice chips to suck on? You're still listed as nil by mouth, but he said you can start on liquids later tonight if you continue to improve."

"Yeah, that would be great. My mouth is so dry that I can barely swallow," she whispered.

Nurse Sarah removed the gloves as she left the room, returning with a cup of crushed ice chips. She sat down on the side of the bed and spoon fed small amounts into Zandra's mouth.

Zandra moaned as the ice melted in seconds on her hot, parched tongue. The cool liquid evaporated before it could put out the fire in the back of her throat. She opened her mouth to ask for more but Nurse Sarah was already there waiting. She gave her two more small amounts then stated, "Best not to overdo it."

She was no longer trying to breathe past razor blades and flames. She let herself surrender to her drug induced exhaustion.

Destiny awoke after one of the most peaceful sleeps he had ever had and smiled to himself. He had never had anyone to call his own, but he did now. The way she had touched him made him feel revitalized, he felt alive for the first time ever. He reached out for his female, but as he stretched, he found that he was alone. He flexed his senses. He couldn't locate her energy anywhere. She was gone. He sat bolt upright in his bed, threw the sheet off and lunged out of bed. Where was she? He checked the locks he'd placed on his realm, all were still secure. Had someone entered while he slept and taken her? Had he lowered his barriers with complacency and allowed entry while he was asleep? Who would take her? Nobody knew she was here, except...

"Death, you've gone too far this time little brother," he growled as he shoved his legs into a pair of black leathers. Next he was pushing his arms through the wholes of a black muscle shirt. Rage rolled off his shoulders as he grabbed a black leather jacket and steel cap shit kickers.

His brother had no right sneaking into his home and taking what he had claimed. If he'd tainted her, he would have no hesitation in rendering a death blow, sending him home to mother in a burning body bag. He finished tying his laces and stormed to his library. There he dug through the drawer of his desk where found his brother's amulet. Holding it in his palm, he wrapped the leather around his fist.

His brother must have brass balls to enter his dominion and take Enigma from right under his nose. By the time he was finished with him, those brass balls would be hanging over the mantel.

He disappeared from his library to solidify in his brother's den. He knew that entering Death's realm without announcing himself was an act of aggression, but he didn't care for niceties in his present state of rage.

His brother's presence swiftly filled the room. He spun on his heel to face the centre of Death's energy. "WHAT HAVE YOU DONE WITH HER? WHERE IS SHE?" he yelled.

"Brother mine, it has been a very long time since you ventured from your realm.

I find your accusations both unwarranted and undesired, not to mention unfounded. I have taken nothing belonging to you," Death dismissed his brother's rantings.

Destiny was on top of Death, his hand around his throat, pinning him to the wall. He didn't know his brother could move that fast. Destiny snarled next to his ear, "You will tell me what you did with her, or I will strangle you with your own entrails."

Death respected the eldest of his brothers. He would walk through the pits of hell and back for him, but he would not tolerate being threatened in his own dimension over something he knew absolutely nothing about.

"ENOUGH!" he yelled, throwing out his power at Destiny. Destiny was blasted backwards by the impact, landing hard on the marble desk that occupied his brother's den.

He had forgotten that Death had always been a worthy opponent when growing up though they hadn't sparred since first coming into their powers. He remembered how they had always been so evenly matched, they could fight for hours and still neither would win the upper hand.

He rolled off the desk top into a defensive crouch. "Again, I ask you, as my brother, where is my female?" Destiny demanded.

Death replied, "As your brother, I do not lie when I say I don't know what you're talking about."

Destiny ran his fingers through his hair in frustration. "If you didn't come to my realm and take her from me, then who? You are the only one that knew she was there. I saw the way you looked upon her. You wanted her! I presumed you had come back after I had claimed her. I thought I sensed in you that you wanted her."

Death shrugged his shoulder, "I was more intrigued by her, than wanting her. She was a pretty sight, laid out on your couch." He raised his hands in surrender at the growl emanating from his big brother's throat. "Hey, I mean no disrespect bro. I was not about to claim what wasn't mine to do so."

Destiny stood to his full height and considered his brother's words. Death was not his enemy in this, and if he was going to find the missing part of his soul, then he would need all the help he could get.

He would have to save face and apologize, but if it meant finding her, he would do all it took. He started, "I am sorry. I thought the worst of you. But when I woke and found she wasn't with me, I guess I went a little crazy." He ran his fingers through his hair. Feeling helpless was not something he handled well. "I don't know where to start looking. I don't even know her name."

Death frowned, "You called her Enigma, and I thought that you must have acquired her name before bedding her?" Death thought to himself, 'Could this possibly get any more complicated than it already was?' Destiny explained all of what had happened after Enigma had woken and the link to the puzzling name.

"Well, I guess we are going to have to try to find her in the human world. You do know that's a needle in a haystack?" Death was not liking the odds of ever finding her, but he was not about to push his big brother's buttons with the unfathomable odds.

"If it means walking every street in every country, I will find her," Destiny said out of desperation. He felt like he couldn't breathe, his chest ached.

Death suddenly had an idea. He didn't know if it would work but it was worth a try. He grabbed his brothers' arm, "Did she leave anything belonging to her in your realm?" Destiny vanished with his brother to his library, "Look around. See if there's anything where we found her." He left his brother to search the library while he made his way to his private bathroom. He knew she'd been wearing clothes that were left discarded after her shower. He found them and returned to the library. "She left these. Now what?" he asked his brother.

"Now I take them to a woman I know of. She has abilities that might help us find her." He almost felt shame in using his brother's circumstances, but he wasn't above using any excuse to see his Vanessa.

CHAPTER 8

"Hey, my gorgeous girl! How are you doing today?" JT said as she entered the hospital room. "Good to see you haven't left the land of the living. I will be your designated driver today, so you better be ready to buckle up babe." She kissed Zandra's cheek

"They seem happy enough to let me go home. Can't stress how good that sounds." She was sitting in the chair next to her bed. She had showered herself and dressed in some soft yoga pants and a T-shirt, with her flip flops. JT must have brought a bag from her home. It was good to finally have all her bandaging off, and she was looking forward to some alone time in her own space. Her movements were still a little restricted by the remaining bruises, but she was confident that she could manage. There would be some things that she would have to become accustomed to, the biggest hurdle being that her sight was still FUBAR.

"Could you take the flowers out to the nurse's station? I don't want to take them home," she asked.

JT looked at the cards to see who'd sent them. One was from an old work colleague and the other garish one was from the bottom feeder, Anne.

She kept the cards and carried the vases out to the nurse's station. "Zandra asked me to leave the flowers here to say thanks ladies, for all you've done for her," she spoke mostly to the blonde, Nurse Sarah, "I'm not sure she's ready to go home, but I guess we will see."

Nurse Sarah walked around the curve of the Nurse's station and held her hand out. In between two fingers she had a card, "Give me a call if you need me. I can always drop by." Sarah had liked JT from the moment she had come to visit Zandra. They had fallen into easy conversation while Zandra had been unconscious. They had started flirting with each other at every visit. Now that Zandra was well enough to go home, Sarah was no longer required to keep it professional. She wanted to see if they could be friends or even more that would be nice too. "Give me a call later and let me know how she settled in. She is going to have some major adjustments to make."

JT slid the card into the pocket of her jeans, "I will. What time suit you for me to call?" she asked wondering what Nurse Sarah looked like with her hair down and in a pair of regular jeans and top. Sarah smiled, "I finish in about two hours. Any time after that is good. If you ring and I don't answer, please leave a message. I'll either be driving or I could be in the shower. I will call back if I know it's you."

"Sure, will do. Better get moving, I think Zandra's eager to kick this joint, she's over the taste of hospital food." She started back to the room where Zandra was waiting with her bag. She could hear one of the nurses say to Sarah, "So you think she'll call?" Sarah sighed, "I hope so. It's been a long time since I met someone like JT."

"Alrighty then, let's get you home, settled and comfortable, shall we?" She raised her hand to help Zandra out of the chair and linked her hand over her arm. She lifted the bag off the bed and they slowly walked out of the room that she had spent the past two weeks visiting every day since the accident.

JT had put in for holidays when she knew Zandra would be coming home. She had spent the weekend at the hospital talking with Nurse Sarah about what kind of modifications would need to be made for her friend. She had then spent the rest of the week preparing for her friend's return home.

JT pressed the button for the lift and waited. The doors opened with a ding. She guided Zandra through the doors and pressed the button to take them to the ground floor. The lift stopped and JT led Zandra to her black SUV parked in the pickup zone. Not too soon either as a parking attendant was just about to give her a ticket. Asshole!

~

Death had materialized at Vanessa's place. The apartment indicated that she was still residing there. It had taken him months to locate her whereabouts this time. It was always like a cat-and-mouse game between them, that neither one wanted to delve into too deeply. He had not openly let her know he had found her this time, but for his brother he would do what he could. If that meant having to find her again then so be it.

He followed the hall to the space where she slept. He inhaled her scent deep into his lungs and grew restless with every breath. He knew he was being sick and twisted, but he couldn't help himself. He lifted her pillow in both hands and smothered his face. Her natural fragrance was intoxicating. It would leave him aching from a torture buried deep, caused by years of struggling with this woman. He threw the pillow back on the bed disgusted by his own weakness, steadied himself and then vanished.

Death materialized in the empty elevator at the hospital he had found Vanessa in two months ago when he had come to claim a mark on his list. She hadn't seen him as she exited the room of one mean old son of a bitch. Seth Grey's date and time had come. His destiny had been to develop liver cancer after being an alcoholic for the majority of his life. He had been a bastard to his high school sweetheart that had given him two children. She protected her kids against the man who was content to blame all things bad on them. He would frequently get drunk and Penny would put herself between her offspring and the drunken prick who was supposed to be her Prince Charming. The kids had grown up and moved out and Penny had died from a heart attack. Seth's children had not spoken to him since the day of their mother's death. Seth only had the companionship from a bottle of cheap whiskey to keep him warm at night, and even that had been his downfall. One's like Seth left him feeling sick to his soul, their essence sour and distasteful. Even after all this time, he had to convince his gag reflex not to react to the bitter aftertaste.

He placed his hands on the shoulders of Seth Grey, hoping that the morphine dripping into his system would not deny him his painful grip. Seth opened his eyes to come face to face with his demise. Death bent down beside the old man's ear and whispered, "Your last breath is measured by the integrity of which you lived. Expect pain old man." Pulling back he placed the kiss of death to Seth's forehead then inhaled the old man's last breath. He was too weak to hang on for long, his body eaten away by cancer. He knew his time was up, and then his eyes faded, gone.

Death had stood, wiped his mouth with back of his hand, and rubbed the palm of his hand up and down his chest with the sensation of eating something bad. He grimaced and started to disappear, but as the door started to open he faltered, only dimming enough to watch from the corner of the room. Vanessa came in, checked Seth's vitals and hit the button on the wall before starting to make notes on the chart. Seth had signed a do not resuscitate order. Wouldn't have made any difference, there was no coming back for Seth Grey. Not from where he was going. His only purpose in life had been to donate the sperm for offspring that would go on to be significant in their time. Other than that his life had no impact and definitely not one worth saving. He did owe Seth Grey one thank you very much, he had led him to Vanessa. After several long months and much duty, he had at last found her again.

The elevator doors opened with a ding and he strode down the hall to the nurse's station. The blonde sitting behind the desk looked up and flushed, "Can I help you sir?"

Death gave a slight nod, "I'm looking for Nurse Vanessa. Nurse Sue, can you tell me where I might find her? "The blonde's name tag baptized her as Nurse Sue Flanagan, installing familiarity in hope of creating less of a scene. "I'm an old friend who only just found out that she's working here."

She stood to get a better look at the eye candy and his wrappings. He had on black leathers, a black muscle shirt, black leather duster and black sunglasses. After a few seconds, Nurse Sue came out of her gaze of appreciation of the male specimen standing in front of her. She looked over her shoulder and said, "She's just finished her hand over for change of shift. She will be in the locker room getting ready to leave." He thanked her and left via the elevator he had arrived in. He decided to wait at the entry doors to the hospital, invisible to all. He didn't want her to run again before he had a chance to speak with her.

Vanessa was tired - it had been a long shift. One of the other Nurses had called in sick. All she wanted to do was get home, soak in a hot bath and read her book until the water got cold. She dug in her handbag for keys to her black Capri. As she put her hand on her keys in the bottom of her bag, she looked around with the uneasy sense of being watched. Maybe it was her usual paranoia. She had been here for about six months, and she would have to start making plans to move on soon, before he could find her again.

CHAPTER 9

JT used her spare set of keys to open the door to Zandra's two-bedroom apartment, then led her in. "Now, until you get familiar with where things are and moving around in here, I've moved a couple of things so you don't bump into them. I moved the side board you had here in the front entry. So if you try to put your keys or bag on it, it'll land on the floor. I've put your coat rack next to the door you can hang your bag on that. I've put a hook next to the door hinge for you to hang your keys so you don't lose them. All of this is temporary mind you, you'll have your sight back in no time I'm sure. Listen to me rambling." JT had heard the doctors say that her sight would be unpredictable. That it could be days, weeks, months or maybe never due to swelling and damage to nerves in and around her eyes. There was always hope.

Leading her friend into the living room, she continued to point out the changes and modifications that had been made to make adjusting to her new life easier. She had automatic timers put in for lights, so that people knew someone was home. Zandra and JT had gone head to head about Zandra staying on her own after JT had said she was moving in for a while. Zandra stood her ground, needing to re-establish her independence, so to keep the situation from getting out of hand, JT had graciously pulled her head in on the subject. The modification made JT feel better about caving in. The neighbourhood wasn't a rough one, but nobody could rule out break and enters in the economic climate happening with the new change in government. Shutters had been installed on a timer to prevent access of unwanted intrusion (of the human kind) and excess light exposure. Until her friend's eyes were in full working order again, JT had taken every precaution when it came to safety. She had added extra locks to both the front and back doors along with chains. Okay, so she may have gone a little overkill, but hey, it was the only way to know that her friend was safe when she wasn't around.

JT informed Zandra, "I've stocked up the fridge and freezer. You have plenty of chocolate mud ice cream, and if there's anything you need that you are out of I can always shop and drop for you."

"I know you normally like to have a drink and relax with a good book, so I took the liberty of getting you credit for your iTunes. I thought you might be able to survive with some audio books, at least until things improve. If I'm over stepping the line, just let me know and I'll back off."

"JT stop. Breathe for me. You're doing my head in. Relax, the doctor said not to stress too much over the small things. You've been my rock through all this and I still have a long way to go. I will get you to fine tune a few things for me that I need on a daily basis, but I will get through this. I'm not about to give up, but I also have to be realistic in case this is my world now." All she wanted to do now was climb into her king size bed and sleep for the next week. Maybe she would wake up to find this was all just a really bad dream.

"Are you hungry, can I get you anything?" JT offered, "I got some of that coffee you like or there's cold drinks in the fridge?"

Running her hands up and down her thighs she said, "I think I'm good. I might just have a lay down for a while." She made her way down the hall, stripped off her clothes and climbed into bed. Nothing felt as good as her own pillow as she closed her eyes and drifted off to sleep.

She dreamed of waking up in a library full of books, in a house she had never seen before. There was the most gorgeous man with black hair and dark eyes, which held a lonely sadness. Her body was on fire for this stranger, her body heating, aching to touch him. She wanted to soothe the sadness, take away his loneliness. She wanted to see what his smile looked like. Then he was kissing her, and she moaned with the taste of him. Someone was calling her name, "Zandra, Zandra wake up. It's just a dream." It all faded away as her mystery lover pleaded for her to stay. The fog lifted, and she recognized her friend JT's voice saying, "It's just a dream, Zan. It's alright. You're safe. You were moaning in your sleep. You sounded distressed."

Zandra blushed, "I was having a dream, but it wasn't a bad dream."

"Well, sorry about that, I didn't mean to interrupt. I bet it was just getting interesting too," JT laughed apologetically. "So, who was it? Please tell me it wasn't that looser ex of yours?" JT enquired. She had never liked Ethan.

Zandra laughed, "No, Ethan is not raunchy dream worthy. I have no idea who the gorgeous guy was. Maybe my imagination conjured him up. He was too perfect to be real." And if he was, he probably wouldn't go for a chunky woman, at least not with the lights on.

Destiny was pacing back and forth in his library. Death had prevented him from going with him to see the women he called Vanessa. He had said that it would make her uncomfortable working with others around. His brother had been gone for hours and it was all taking longer than his sanity could handle.

The air stirred beside him and his brother, Dream's essence occupied the space to his left. "Morpheus, what are doing here?"

Dream replied, "What, no hello? I missed you too brother. I don't have time for idle chatter, I have questions I need answers to. I'm hoping the answers are in your library. May I have access?" Dreams voice wavered with the sound of desperation.

"Is this something I should be worried about?" he asked as he was the keeper of mankind. He needed to know if the balance within his realm was under threat.

Dream responded, "No brother, this is of a personal nature. It only affects my realm at this time, but it could instigate a ripple in the fold that would eventually reach all of us. Please brother, this is important to me."

Destiny knew Dream was talking in circles trying not to give too much away, but if he denied him access and the ripple reached his realm, the ramifications could be devastating. "Fine, do what you must."

With a relieved thank you, Dream walked into the body of shelving on a mission. Destiny resumed his pacing back and forth in front of his desk.

~

Death partially materialized in Vanessa's flat. He had dropped back and given her space as she left the parking lot. He knew she would eventually get home. He had watched her pull into the garage from a safe distance, undetected. If she saw him before she was locked safe in her apartment, she had a better chance to flee. Once he had given her time to relax in her surroundings, he made his move. He could see and watch her but she couldn't see him.

She walked out of her bedroom wearing a short, red, silk robe. She walked down the hall towards the kitchen with a book in one hand and an empty coffee cup in the other. She had spent the last forty minutes soaking in a hot scented bath. As she entered the kitchen, she opened the fridge, starting to take things out to make dinner. She had taken chicken breast out of the fridge and dug out a couple of saucepans placing one on the stove with water to boil. Cutting the chicken, she placed it in the second saucepan with a little oil to seal it, throwing a little garlic and some Thai herbs in with the chicken. She turned to the pantry, grabbing the Jasmine rice, a can of coconut cream, and some chicken stock, then returned to the stove. Throwing in some rice to cook, she added the stock to the chicken. Stirring it through, she covered it. She knew it would have been easier to just go with a five minute microwave dinner, but she liked the taste of her own cooking better. It didn't have that plastic aftertaste. She took a bowl out of the cupboard and a spoon from the drawer.

She browsed the TV menu to see if anything was worth watching, but nothing jumped out at her. She switched off the TV and flicked on her iPod docking station connected to her surround sound. She would settle for her book and some music to feed her soul while she fed her hunger.

She returned to the stove, added the coconut cream to the chicken, stirred and replaced the lid. She rinsed the rice, covered it in foil and let it drain. She took a soda and her book to the table. She returned to the kitchen, spooned some rice into her bowl and topped it with the green Thai curry. Making sure everything was turned off, she took the spoon and bowl to the table. She opened her soda, picked up her book, and opening it at her page, she began to eat.

Death could not take any more waiting. He fully materialized at the other end of the table and watched Vanessa freeze with her loaded spoon half way to her open mouth as she paled.

Death raised both his hands open-palmed in a non-threatening way. "Vanessa, I'm not here to hurt you, I mean you no harm. I need your help." His eyes focused on her open mouth and he wondered what it would feel like to kiss those soft plump lips.

Oh my God, he'd found her again! She knew it wasn't safe staying in one place for so long, but she had really liked it here. She thought she'd felt him earlier. It didn't pay to become complacent.

Death waited for her to say something, anything, but he was watching her face play out her reaction to him barging into her home uninvited. First there was shock, quickly replaced by anger, then a sadness that reached him bone deep.

"What do you want? And if I help you, will you leave me alone?" She would need to leave as soon as she had a chance.

Death explained he needed her talents with the craft to find someone. He only had a dress, a pair of shoes and a hairpin.

She told him to leave the stuff on the chair at the end of the table and come back in a couple of hours. She was in the middle of dinner. She was not happy watching him shake his head back and forth, he was here till he got what he wanted from her.

Death didn't trust her not to run, and he really needed the information. He knew his brother would be going crazy waiting. He wasn't going anywhere. He walked to the kitchen and taking a bowl out of the cupboard, he spooned some rice and chicken into it. He turned to the fridge, grabbing a soda and a fork from the drawer on the way past. He moved to the table and sat beside her.

Vanessa watched as the bastard really made himself at home. Strangely she did not want to think about how his company soothed her raw edges. She couldn't afford that kind of energy.

~

Dream had given up looking for now as he didn't seem to be able to find whatever it was he was searching for.

Destiny had long worn a tread in the carpet in front of his desk. He had tried to focus on his duties but he just couldn't. In the end he had opted for having something to eat, a shower and trying to get some sleep. Maybe things would happen quicker if he wasn't counting the seconds, minutes or hours since he'd woken to find his female gone.

He undressed, opened the shower door and stepped in turning the water on hot. He closed his useless eyes and let the water run over his head. The sensation of the water on his body instantly reminded him of a warm soft body sliding over his skin. His memory replayed their time in the shower. He was clenching and releasing his fists next to his thighs. He refused to touch himself. It wouldn't compare and his soul couldn't take any further torture. He washed himself quickly, turned the shower off and dried himself like it was a business arrangement. Then he stomped to his bed, threw the covers back and climbed in. The bed felt too big without her in it. As he placed his head on the pillow, there was a lump digging into his cheek. Lifting his head his hand found a small pouch.

Dream had said thanks for allowing access to his library with the gift of sand. This meant he could use the sand to dream about his female, his beautiful Enigma. He may be able to find her in the dream realm with the help of his brother.

"Thanks Sandman," he chuckled, his hopes sparked back to life. He wondered if his brother Morpheus even knew how precious his gift was at the moment. If it worked, he made a promise to offer aid to Dream if ever he needed it.

CHAPTER 10

Destiny dipped his thumb in the pouch and then lifted it to his forehead. Without the care to measure it out, he placed his thumb between his brows, leaving a sandy print. If he slept for a week, he didn't give a shit as long as he slept with his woman curled against his chest. He closed his eyes and tried to relax, with his last thought being there was a storm blowing outside. He was sucked down into the dream vortex, like he'd been hit upside the head with a lump of four by two.

Zandra had spent a good half hour soaking in a hot bath after dinner. It helped her to relax, easing some of the residual aches and pains from the car accident. She may not have her sight back but that was small, compared to mortality. The car that had ploughed into her had two fatalities, one at the site and the other had died en-route to the hospital. With those odds, learning to live with never being able to see again, was something she had come to peace with. The only thing she would really miss was driving her red Audi, anywhere, any time. The insurance money would buy her time when it came to work, so there was no pressure there. She smiled to herself, which in itself was a small blessing. She laughed, "No more working for that bitch." She climbed out of the bath, removed the clip from her hair and towelled off. She walked out of the bathroom and felt her way to the bed. Climbing in, she relished the feel of her thousand thread count sheets on her skin. She was much more comfortable in her own bed.

JT had, under protest, gone on a supper date with Nurse Sarah after much coer-

cion. It would be nice for JT to find someone. The last couple of women she had
dated had been, for want of a better word,
psychotic.

She closed her eyes and drifted off to
sleep, thinking about a gorgeous dark
haired man that was built like a Greek
Adonis. He was standing in a kitchen, his
chest was bare, his black sweat pants
riding low on his hips. His arms were
crossed over his chest, his brows were
drawn down and he did not look happy.
She was too busy admiring his body to
hear what he was saying. He grabbed her
with a speed that was not humanly possible and had her hands behind her back.
Her breasts rose in his face, and he
brushed his lips over hers, plundering her
mouth, claiming it.

Her breath was coming fast and heated
as he lifted her naked ass to the bench top.
He relinquished her mouth only long
enough to remove the black shirt she was
wearing, throwing it to the bench beside
her. He wedged himself as close as he
could, his material covered hardness

resting against her cleft. His lips moved along her jaw to her ear and he whispered softly, "I need to taste the fruit from your garden. It smells fragrant and ripe to eat." His lips trailed down her neck, his tongue finding her hardened nipple. He rolled it in his mouth like he was sucking the flesh off a ripe cherry seed. He moved from one painfully hard nipple to the other to lavish it with his tongue. He trailed his tongue down the centre of her body, circling her navel. He had her breathless with anticipation.

He placed his hand between her breasts and lightly encouraged her to recline back onto the bench. She accommodated his silent request, too on fire to protest. He lifted her legs over his shoulders and kissed her inner thighs. She was squirming with desire, needing him to douse the flames building in her aching pussy. His thumbs opened her lips, exposing her inner heat, as his head dipped. His tongue penetrated her inner frills to slide from her core to her clit. He repeated the motion several times, each time thrusting his tongue inside her canal. "Please, I can't take it, it's too much. I need to cum," she begged, her head rolling sideways back and forth, her hand sinking into his hair to increase the pressure. Her hips lifted to meet his manipulations. She ached for him, more than ever before in her life. He slid a thick finger into her hot wet pussy as he circled his intentions around her nub.

He wrapped his arm around her thigh to open her up with his forefinger and middle finger, the hood sliding up, exposing the sensitive nerves in her swollen bud. As he placed his mouth over her most sensitive bit and used his tongue to gently suckle, he started to glide two fingers into her inferno. Her back arched and her orgasm had her star struck, her eyes rolled back in her head, and her entire body was pulsing in sync with the heart beat in her bud.

As her body thrummed, she felt the smoothness of his hard cock slide along her wetness. In one plunge he was buried balls deep, and a second orgasm rolled over her and through her as the head nudged the end of her vault. He rolled his hips as he slid back, leaving only the bulbous head nuzzled at her opening. With no time to recover from over sensitive nerves, her body oozed hot juices over his shaft, as he drove it home again. He set a slow and torturous pace that had her gasping for air. As he withdrew, she inhaled and as he seated himself deep, she exhaled. As he grew harder inside her, he increased the rhythm to a pounding, earth shattering pace.

She was teetering on the edge as he lowered her legs, wrapping them around his waist, he placed his thumb against her already furious clit. "Cum for me," he commanded and her body exploded, her walls milking him violently. He threw his head back and with one last thrust, he released his load, "Arrrrrgh."

Destiny woke covered in sweat, gasping for air, his entire body throbbing. He reached out to the bed beside him, it was empty. His chest aching, he rolled to his side, his seed running across his stomach. He gathered the pillow she'd used from her side of the bed and cradled it to his chest. He didn't know how long it would take to find her but he would never stop searching.

Zandra woke with the sheets tangled around her legs, her body throbbing. Her pussy was pulsating and her clit buzzing. She ran her hand down over her breasts, her nipples were diamond hard. Her hand following the mid-line of her body to her swollen lips, she slipped her middle finger through her slit. She met with a puddle of wetness, "Damn, that's horny." She couldn't resist circling her swollen bud as she relived what her mysterious dream man had done to her.

She opened the drawer to her bedside table, removing her glass dildo from its pouch. She placed the pillow from beside her and laid it under her knees. Running the cool dildo along her heated centre, she slid the head inside, then ran it up over her bud, like he was using his tongue. She then thrust it deep, and holding it in place with her inner muscles, she moved the pillow into place. The pillow against her cheeks stopped her body expelling the dildo before her pussy could suck it back inside.

Her middle finger finding her juices, she teased her clit, her hips rolling her ass against the pillow. She was shameless, she needed to orgasm, and her dream man was not around to take care of the physical. With her mind picturing his body suspended above her, his hips meeting hers, she came hard and fast. Her heart pounding from her orgasm, she removed the pillow, her pulsing pussy expelling her dildo. She placed it carefully on the bedside table, rolled over and went back to sleep, saddened by the thought she had no idea who the guy in her dreams was, knowing that if she didn't get her sight back, she had no way to find him. She could walk past him in the street and never know.

Destiny sat at his desk with his head in his hands, he had not touched his duties. He couldn't. All he kept thinking about was the emptiness surrounding him. There was no warmth, no peace. Inside him there had been a storm brewing since he woke to find his female had vanished.

The surrounding air shifted in the room, the temperature took on a warm breeze with floral fragrance. He inhaled the warm loving aura of his mother's love. Cosmo solidified dressed in her full ethereal robes.

"What pains you my eldest? I feel your despair and your imbalance within. How can I ease your soul? It's unsettling to me. You are usually so stable compared to your brothers and sisters," she inquired. The sound of her voice held sadness. As an empath she could always sense her children's internal struggles.

Destiny lifted his head, "Mother, I am sorry to burden you. It was not my intent."

Cosmo replied, "You are normally so committed to your duties, but of late, you seem to be unhappy with your role. What troubles you so?"

Destiny knew he had to choose his words with care, he loved his mother. Showing disrespect would not bode well and could hinder his wishes. "I am disheartened. I have been in charge of the human race's fate since becoming of age. You know I take my responsibilities extremely seriously, however, recently I had an experience that has left me feeling at odds with the men and women affected by the Realm of Destiny." He paused. Sighing, he continued, in for a penny in for a pound. "I know that men and women have children. They grow up, meet someone, have ceremonies and live together, their destinies overlapping, creating new life and the cycle continues."

"What does this have to do with your inner turmoil?" Cosmo asked.

Destiny responded in the simplest formulae of words he could conjure, "I am lonely mother. I do not understand why they should have someone to complete their souls, yet we are trapped in our realms, alone, day after day, week after week, and year after year. I need more out of my existence. I can't just leave here. I don't have the luxury of seeing and travelling the world. I only keep in touch with Death as our realms share responsibilities. I rarely see any of my brothers or sisters unless they want or need something from me."

"I had no idea you were so disconnected. I am sorry that I have only visited on the rare occasion that I sensed your need for me. I will try to do better in the future."

Destiny had the distinct impression that his mother was not really getting his point. To verify and confirm the view from where he was, he said, "Mother, I am trying to explain to you. I need more than my kin. I want a female to share my realm with. One who will be mine."

"What if I was to tell you that there is someone who has the other half of your soul? That she is in charge of her own destiny and that you would have to find her and win her heart? I would give you a week's reprieve of your duties, but it would be like finding a needle in a haystack. You will need to go to her world and live as a man and win her as such. You cannot use your influence as Destiny to persuade her as she is immune. What would you say?"

Destiny didn't even think about it, "Sign me up."

Cosmo sighed shaking her head, "You know you will be on a time limit and you must return according to our agreement, either with or without her?"

Destiny already knew that he had met his female. He just needed to find her. "What if I fail to return with her?"

"Are you willing to fail before you have even tried? I cannot offer more than that at this time. I do, however, give you my blessing." Cosmo knew that this was her son's battle and lesson to learn. If she handed Destiny his fated, he may under appreciate the enormity of his test. "I will give you one parting gift. While on sabbatical, I will give you sight while in the human realm. The minute you leave here, the sand in this glass starts to flow. It flows one way and there is no way to reverse it or slow it down. Once all the sand has emptied, you will be required to return. If you do not return, you will be summoned. If you refuse to answer the summons, you will be exiled. Do you understand the depths of which your venture demands?" With one hand on either cheek she drew her son to level. Cosmo placed a kiss on his forehead as Destiny nodded, "Yes, Mother. Thank you." She swiftly withdrew her hold and was gone on a whisper of warm breeze.

Cosmo returned to her realm of creation. She sat down hard in the chair in her study. She knew this time had been fast approaching. She looked down at the open journal on her desk, and with a little smile replaced the gold ribbon as a book mark. The words on the pages were blurred as a tear ran down her cheek which she brushed away with the back of her hand. She picked up the book, closed it and walked to the shelves. She slid it back onto the shelf next to Death's journal. She gently ran her fingers along the spine with the loving touch of a mother.

She removed Death's journal from the shelf and returned to her desk. Sighing to herself, she slowly sank down into her seat, as she opened it to the place marked by a gold ribbon.

Destiny was in a state of shock. He had actually wondered if the conversation he'd just had with his mother had transpired. Maybe he'd been too heavy handed with his brother's dream sand and he was still in the dream realm.

He would have pinched himself to check, but that was just stupid. There was no way to know if he was pinching himself in his dream or in reality.

He couldn't sit still, he had to move around. He started pacing back and forth in front of his desk. After the third cycle, he kept walking and was through the door, heading for his bedroom. He grabbed several changes of clothes and toiletries, and secured the pouch of dream sand and the hourglass, loading them into a duffel bag. Everything was ready to go the minute his brother returned with information. Destiny swore under his breath, "Where the fuck are you?" He was eager to get this shit happening as in yesterday. His own future depended on it.

CHAPTER 12

Zandra had started the day out feeling disjointed. She felt like a caged tiger. She had woken early according to her talking clock. It was saying it was only half-past six. She got dressed into her yoga pants and a sports bra. She took the iPod off the docking station next to the bed, then hit play after plugging in her headphones and clipping it to the waist of her pants. She felt her way along the hall to the living room, turning right at the corner and raising her hand in front of herself so as not to run into the treadmill. Her hand came into contact with the bar, so she let go of the wall and followed the bar around. Stepping up onto the mat, she smiled as her hand ran over the flat control panel. JT had stuck a raised dot on the start button, two dots on the stop. There was an arrow pointing upwards for faster and one pointing downwards to go slower. Her friend was priceless. She pressed the dot for the go button and the mat started to move. As she started to increase the speed, she kept her other hand on the bar so as not to lose her balance.

Music blaring in her ears, she started to stomp out all of her frustration. She thought back to the morning of the party, remembering the text message she had received from Ethan.

Hi Zandra,
This thing with us isn't working for me. I've met someone else.
Ethan

She thought, REALLY? What kind of bastard was he? He didn't even have the balls to call her and tell her. Granted they had only been seeing each other for a couple of months, but a text message? It was the principle of it. She knew it wasn't working for her either. There was just something unsettling about him. She came to the solid conclusion that he wasn't worth losing sleep over, thinking that maybe karma would have his ass dumped by text one day. She smiled to herself while breathing heavily from striding it out.

She suddenly felt like she was being watched and the hairs on the back of her neck stood up. She ripped the earphones off and threw them over her shoulder. She started feeling for the stop button while calling out, "Is someone there? JT is that you?" Feeling anxious she found the emergency stop cord and pulled it. The mat stopped moving immediately, her footing unsteady she stepped off. Feeling her way along the bar, she made her way to the wall. With her back to the wall, she side stepped to the corner and followed the turn, eager to reach the bedroom. The bedroom door had a lock on it, as did the bathroom door, if she could make it. There was a movement of air without sound to her right. She held her breath for a moment, trying to recall her self-defense lessons, then with tired legs she ran along the hall and into her room, slamming her door. She locked it and slid down, knees braced, back against the door, as she put her head on her arms and listened. She knew it wasn't JT, she would have answered her, and nobody else had a key. Ethan and she hadn't gone that far in their relationship as to swap keys.

After waiting for several minutes, she broke into a hysterical fit of laughter, followed shortly thereafter by tears. Sliding sideways, she crumpled on the floor sobbing. She was fractured, broken. What would she do if her sight didn't come back? She hated feeling sorry for herself and up till now she hadn't allowed herself to even think of all the things she would miss.

She would no longer be able to go shopping and buy shoes that matched her clothes. She would always have to go with a friend and hope it was a good day, or she could walk out wearing a potato sack with grandma flowers in purple and orange. She would no longer be able to watch and appreciate the graphics in a movie. She wouldn't be able to sit and read a book or flip through a magazine. She felt absolutely exhausted after her pity party. She wiped her tears away from her useless eyes and pushed herself up. She was obviously having some kind of breakdown. She stumbled her way to the bathroom and followed the bench to the toilet. Lifting the lid, she lost the meager contents of her stomach.

She was pretty certain that if there was someone in the apartment, they would have made themselves known to her. Chalking it all up to an over active imagination and the stress of the past few weeks, she removed her clothing. She opened the shower door and turned on the water. She needed to wash away the sweat and tears. She stepped in and closed the door and turning her back to the water, leaned her head back and let the water drown out her sorrows.

As she rinsed her hair of conditioner, she took the sponge from its hook, soaped it up and started to wash her arms. As she washed her neck and shoulders, the water and suds caressed her nipples, like a lover's touch. In her mind, she saw a tall handsome man with black hair and black eyes, his strong jaw framing full lips, lips that you could kiss for days before coming up for air. She wished she knew who he was. She had no way of finding him now. "One day at a time," she sighed.

Death had used the directions Vanessa had given him to find Destiny's female. He had only partially formed in her living room and was watching her. He knew something was off when she removed her earphones and asked if someone was there. She couldn't know he was there, he was invisible.

She seemed to become panicked and anxious, stopping the machine so abruptly that she almost lost her footing. He moved to stabilize her before her own momentum could hurt her. She felt her way along the bar, and then with her back to the wall, she had stepped sideways along it to the corner. He thought to show himself to reassure her that everything was fine. Solidifying a short distance from her, he was shocked to realize that her eyes looked right through him. He took a step closer and lifting his hand, he waved it in front of her. She suddenly broke from her frozen stance to run toward the room at the end of the hall. He heard the lock flick as he just stood there in a state of shock. She couldn't see him. He'd seen his brother's blind stare all his life. He knew that his brother's female did not have the gift of sight.

His chest hurt for his brother. How was he going to tell him? He cursed under his breath. He was about to leave when he heard the female laugh. Okay, now his interest had been sparked, what was so funny? He semi-formed in the room behind the closed door. She was slumped on the floor sobbing and he was at a loss of what to do. His brother's female looked to be in a world of pain. His fists clenched and opened at his sides. He didn't know how long he stood there, but as his brain tried to find a solution, she pushed herself up and staggered to the attached bathroom. He moved to keep a visual, needing to confirm that she was all right. She started to heave the contents from her stomach. The compassion he felt for his brother was overwhelming, Destiny's female was sick. After ensuring that she had recovered enough to consider a shower, he left.

CHAPTER 13

Death materialised in front of his brother's desk. He lifted his head as he registered the despair rolling off him. Destiny sprang to his feet, "Did you find her?"

Death clenched and unclenched his jaw, "Yes." That answer cost Death more than anything. The information he obtained from Vanessa had come at a high price, and for his brother, he had signed on the dotted line. He turned to the couch and sat down, his elbows on his knees and his head in his hands. Where to start? "There are some complications you need to know about."

Destiny didn't care, "Fuck the complications," he demanded, "take me to her."

Death sighed, "Brother, you need to be aware of the situation."

Destiny stopped short from lighting his internal fuse. He hadn't even considered any type of blockades that might stop him from claiming what was his. One thought in particular had never crossed his mind. "Does she have entanglements with another male?" he growled the words through clenched teeth.

Death explained that he had gone to the apartment, and that she was the same female that had appeared on the couch. He relayed all his observations and his concern for the female being sick. He also added that the woman's apartment showed no signs of any male cohabitation.

Destiny knew that with everything his mother had said and done, that regardless of his female's circumstances, he had to be there. She needed him and he wouldn't let anything happen to her.

Destiny stormed over to a duffel bag next to his desk, threw it over his shoulder and was done thinking and talking. He needed to be action in motion, for the sake of his sanity. "Take me to her," he commanded.

"You're in luck. The apartment next to hers is empty. Do you think you can work with that?" Death offered. After his brother gave a quick nod, he moved to stand beside him. Placing a hand on his Destiny's shoulder, he sarcastically clicked his heels twice saying, "There's no place like home. Follow me," as they melted away.

One minute later, Destiny was standing in a modestly furnished apartment, a little disoriented, but in one piece, his vision swimming. He closed his eyes for a moment, then opened them slowly. It was like his brain had exploded in a techno-colored rainbow migraine. He held his breath while his stomach protested as the nausea receded slowly. He exhaled the breath he'd been holding. He was damn sure he didn't want to do that too often. He lifted his hands to look at the back of them and turned them over a couple of times, to be certain he was actually seeing what he was seeing through his own eyes.

He turned to his brother, grabbed him in a bear hug and clapped him on the back. Excitement buzzed through him. It was exhilarating to be able to see for himself.

Death was taken aback by his brother's actions. He was trying to process what was happening. When his brother pulled back, he glanced at Destiny questionably. That's when he noticed the change in his brother's eyes. No longer vacant and glassy, he now had focus. How could that be? Destiny had always been blind. Destiny smiled broadly, "It's a gift, and I didn't sell my soul or anything."

Death wasn't so sure about that, his brother may be seduced by Earthly beauties. He may not want to return to living in darkness. Shit this could swiftly go south.

He had to act fast to get this show on the road. The longer his brother spent here on Earth, the more he may be reluctant to return to his post.

His parting words to his brother were, "Just press the red button." As his brother disintegrated, he heard an ungodly whaling coming from the apartment next door. He ran to the door, threw it open and raced to the door of the apartment beside his. His fists pounded on it. He needed to shut that contraption up.

After what seemed like ages, the door was opened and standing there was his female. Tears were running down her face, making his heart ache. He yelled over the noise, coming louder now that it wasn't hindered by walls or doors. "Where is it?" She had her fingers plugged into her ears. "It's between the kitchen and the living room. I can't see it to turn it off."

He moved past her into the apartment, grabbed a bar stool near the bench, lifted it up to the ceiling and used one of the legs to push the red button. Silence! His ears were still deafened by the residual buzz. He placed the stool back at the kitchen bench, turned and almost bumped straight into his woman.

She had no idea who her knight in shining armor was, but she was grateful he'd shown up when he did. He ran his hand from the inside of her elbow to her hand, and lifting her hand to his lips, he placed a kiss to her knuckles. "Des Chancellor, at your service my lady. I'm your new neighbour next door. I had just finished moving in when I heard the alarm."

Well flip her over and call her a pancake if his voice wasn't like maple syrup to a sweet tooth. He smelled delicious too. He was still holding her hand, making small circles with his thumb. Tingles wove their way through her veins to her heart. The gate had opened, and the race was on.

Several heartbeats later she found her tongue stuck to the roof of her mouth. Great, she probably appeared mute as well as blind. "Sorry, I'm Zandra. Zandra Wilson. Nice to meet you."

There was something about the man standing in front of her that she found soothing. "Thank you for coming to my rescue." She slid her hand away from him and turned as her voice became shaky. Tears started to run down her face again. Great, the pity party was back in full swing.

Destiny couldn't take his eyes off her. She was the most spectacular thing he'd ever seen, not that he'd seen a lot in his long life, but she was even more beautiful through his own eyes. She had a full figure, curvy in all the right places. Her skin was like alabaster, he loved the way her cheeks had colored. Her hand was so soft and smooth. All he could think about was how it would feel touching him. His body hardened. The smell of her skin when he had placed his kiss to her hand had made him want to taste her all over. He was trapped in his own thoughts as she turned from him. When he heard a sob he snapped, and he wrapped his arms around her from behind. As his head lowered to her ear, he whispered, "Please don't cry. I can't bear it."

She wiped at her face, trying to pull away. She didn't know the first thing about this stranger. She should be more careful, he could be an axe murderer.

As she tried to pull away, he tightened his hold, "Shhh, just let me hold you. Sometimes in life you just need to be held."

Didn't she know it? It had been weeks

since she'd had any interaction with the outside world, apart from her best friend. JT had her own life to live, even though she was steadfast and a true friend. Without JT's help, she hadn't ventured out of her apartment or spoken to anyone else.

She let go as she fell to pieces in the strong arms holding her up. She was a wreck. Embarrassed and feeling sick to her stomach, she pushed away from him, "Oh God, I think I'm going to be sick." She hurriedly made her way to the bathroom, lifted the lid and lost it. In between heaves, she registered her hair was being held, and a hand was rubbing up and down her back gently. Who does that kind of shit? Holding a stranger's hair while they throw up?

She felt as weak as a kitten and staggered to her feet. Regaining her balance with his help, she made her way to the sink. She grappled for a tooth brush and toothpaste and cleaned her teeth. As she stood back up from rinsing her mouth, she started to feel herself list sideways. He had swept her up in his arms, moving swiftly out of the bathroom and was laying her on the bed.

She felt him move away. He must have returned to the bathroom. She heard drawers and cupboards opening and closing, followed by water running. The bed beside her dipped as he sat down, he wiped her face gently with a warm washer, and then placed a cool folded one over her brow. He lifted her hand into his, laying it palm to palm with his own. How could a stranger blanket her with such a sense of being cherished, like she really mattered? She suddenly thought to herself 'He's probably already taken. Why would he be interested in someone like me, wrecked and broken?'

Destiny's heart was beating rapidly out of fear for his female. He didn't know what to do to help her ride out this sickness. Luckily, his instincts kicked in and he tried to ease her discomfort as best he could. If he could have taken her sickness away he would have, but he didn't have that power.

CHAPTER 14

He placed her hand down beside him on the bed and stood. He had made the decision that he wasn't going to leave her alone to fend for herself. If she woke and needed him, he'd be there. So he made his way back to his apartment next door, grabbed a pair of sweat pants and a towel. He grabbed his toiletries bag and made his way back to her apartment. He locked his door as he left, and as he entered hers, he locked the door behind himself.

He headed back through the bedroom into the bathroom, leaving the door open. He stripped off and climbed into a hot shower. It had been a long, stressful day, and he slowly started to unwind, washing it all down the drain.

He towelled his body dry with brisk movements and cleaned his teeth. He shoved his legs into his sweats and tied the string as he re-entered the bedroom. She had only stirred enough to roll onto her side. Not wanting to scare her, he laid down on the other side of the bed. He was content to just be close to her. He laid there just listening to her even breathing before succumbing to sleep.

She was dreaming of her mystery man again, the dream so real she could touch his broad, hairless chest with her fingertips. She followed his washboard stomach down to the little string of hair under his navel until she met a string tie at the waist of his pants. She pulled the knot loose and slid her hand beneath the band. Her hand met with the bulbous head of his swollen staff, running her thumb over the moist drops weeping from it. Her hand surrounded the mass of thick flesh, so large her fingertips didn't meet. She slowly stroked him once, his hips lifting in need, she stroked him twice. He moaned. She licked her lips and was suddenly on her back with his weight on top of her. Her legs were parted and his hardness was firm against her core.

~

Destiny was dreaming. He could feel Zandra's fingertips gently sliding over his skin. They were exploring his body with a lover's touch.

He felt her hand lower to the band of his sweats. She worked below the band, her thumb rubbing over the head of his cock. His breathing became uncontrolled as her hand wrapped around his thickness. She stroked him once, and he moaned. He lifted his hips to meet her next stroke and opened his eyes. In that instant, he woke to feel his dick throbbing in his female's hand. Before he could think clearly, he rolled her beneath him, caging her body.

He was cradled by her pelvis, her heat searing him deep through layers of clothing he wished weren't there.

He leaned his head down to her shoulder and whispered in her ear, "Zandra, wake up sweet thing. You're dreaming." He just barely managed to drag himself to stand and not kiss her.

Zandra gasped with surprise as she became aware that the person she had been touching was her new neighbour. "Umm, Des is that you?" she whispered, barely able to find her voice. God she wished she could see his face right now. What was he doing here?

He let out a sigh and started pacing back and forth. He needed to regain his composure before he had her back underneath him. "Yeah, it's me."

She noticed the sound of his voice was different, deeper with a raspy edge to it. "Are you okay?" she asked, keeping her thoughts to herself. 'Considering I was just feeling you up five different ways till Sunday.'

He continued his pacing, "Yeah, I will

be. Just give me a minute okay." He was breathing heavily.

She opened her mouth and everything just started to tumble out. She told him about the accident, the adjustments she'd had to make and was still making. She told him about how she had been dumped by Ethan via text message the day of the accident, and the crappy boss she had been working for. Then she told him about the dreams that she'd been having since the accident. "So you see, I thought you were him. I thought I was dreaming." While she gushed all her secrets to him, all she kept thinking was, 'He would probably think she was closer to the crazy cat lady than she herself thought.'

He had stopped pacing when she had mentioned her mystery dream lover. Holy mother of the universe, she was talking about him. The way her cheeks flushed and her face lit up had him wanting to tell it from the highest mountain.

"Please say something. Don't just let me sit here rambling. I can't see your face, so I can't tell if you're looking at me like I'm a freak." She was about to go to him when she felt the bed dip next to her.

"You were sick. I didn't want to leave you alone in case you got worse. So after you fell asleep, I went next door grabbed some clothes and had a shower. I then laid down next to you, so I was close if you needed me. I didn't want to frighten you and I did consider the couch but it was too short for me to sleep on," he lied. "If you like I can leave you, if it makes you feel uncomfortable." Again he lied. He was getting quite good at it as they rolled off his tongue, one after another. He hoped that she would ask him to stay. The doors and walls were too much between them. Shit, clothes were too much as far as he was concerned.

"Would you like something to eat? If you think your stomach has settled enough? I could make you some tea." He knew he was trying to distract her, but whatever worked.

She was sitting there looking so confused and lost. He reached out his hand he fingered a strand of hair. Her hair was like silk. He tucked it behind her ear. He ran his thumb over her cheek and she licked her lips nervously. As she opened her mouth to speak, he leaned in and gently brushed his lips over hers.

She felt his soft lips brush hers and she held her breath. It was over way to soon. He had lips you could kiss for days. He leaned his forehead against hers, breathing heavily. He said, "Let me take care of you, let me get to know you. Everything happens for a reason, a season or a lifetime. I believe in fate and destiny, and I think I'm supposed to be right where I am. So will you let me help you?"

She was left speechless. What could she say? She had known this man only a mere few hours and yet she felt like she had known him forever. She had no idea what he looked like, but looks weren't everything.

She caved, "I think I'd like to get to know you too, but right now, I could really do with going back to sleep. I'm really tired and I don't feel real flash." Now that the rush of the moment was over, she could feel her energy failing.

As there was no request for him to leave, he laid back down beside her. It didn't take long for her breathing to become deep and steady. This time he rolled on his side and pulled her into his arms against his chest. She wriggled closer within his hold, and as he breathed her in, he fell asleep.

CHAPTER 15

Destiny woke up with a start. As he felt the warm body next to him, he relaxed. She hadn't gone anywhere. Her head was tucked under his chin, with her hand on his stubbled cheek and her breath tickling his chest. He felt like he was home with her in his arms. An inner peace settled over him and he closed his eyes. He didn't want to break the spell. He'd happily stay like this forever. He just needed her to feel the same way.

He was grateful that after hearing about the car accident, she had come to him. If she hadn't, Death might have claimed her. He may never have had this chance, and he wasn't about to let her get away.

Her thumb started to stroke the fur on his face as she stretched, her thigh coming to rest against his throbbing hardness. It felt like he'd been hard for this woman forever.

"Sorry, I seem to be making a habit of feeling you up," she apologised, but didn't make a move away from him at first.

Embarrassment made her cheeks flush as she lowered her hand from his face and placed it on his chest. She attempted to add some space between them as she disentangled her legs from his. She needed to get up. The spice of his cologne was making her edgy and her blood was starting to boil. She could feel her need tightening her inner muscles, her juices becoming slick in anticipation.

She mentally shook herself. What was she? A teenager without any control of her hormones? 'Grow up and act your age,' she reprimanded herself mentally.

Destiny figured, "Seeing as we have slept together, how about we spend the day getting to know one another? I guess it's a little backwards and upside down, but you did say you wanted to get to know me. I just moved here from interstate. How about you show me around?" He was working on showing Zandra that she still possessed the strength to escape her four wall prison.

"Would you like something to eat for breakfast? I make a very mean eggs," Destiny smiled. He knew she couldn't see his smile but she would hear it in his voice.

At the mention of food, Zandra was running for the bathroom. He was right behind her, holding her hair again. His concern was growing. His female's health was really starting to scare the shit out of him.

"Zandra, sweet thing, you need to see a doctor. You're not well," Destiny said as he put the plug in the bath and started the water.

"I'm sure it's just a bug I've picked up. I'll be fine," she mumbled as she sat down on the cool tiles. She heard the water running and knew he was filling the tub.

God this guy was good. She didn't have the energy to stand in a shower. He helped her out of her clothes. She would have protested, but didn't have the fight in her. He gently lifted her off the tiled floor and into the tub. He rolled a hand towel up and placed it behind her head so she could lay there.

"Will you be all right for a minute while I make a call?" he waited for her to answer. "Mhmm," was all he got, as the tone was an uncertain affirmation. He guessed she was fine for a minute, it wasn't like she was three. He had turned into an overprotective Neanderthal when it came to this woman.

He stepped into his apartment and focused on getting a hold of his mother. "Mother, I really need your help. Can you come to me?"

All he heard was his mother's voice in his head, "What troubles you my son?"

"It's my female, she is sick. How can I make her better?" he begged.

"I am sorry my son, but there is nothing you can do. Her illness can't be cured." Her voice sounded sympathetic and sad.

His knees weakened at the thought that he was permitted to find the other half of his heart and soul, yet with finding her, the fear of losing her was unbearably real.

"All you can do is make her comfortable, my son. Your time there is limited. You will need to return home soon enough. I hope that she will fall in love with you and you bring her home with you where she would be well taken care of." Cosmo could only pray that her son had the strength to do what was right for all.

With that, he disconnected from his mother. He had thought that maybe she would take pity on him that she would know how to fix this dire situation. Instead, he felt his hands were tied, and he was locked in the pits of hell.

He moved back into Zandra's apartment, locking the door behind him. He made his way back into the bathroom, taking a washcloth from the cupboard under the sink. He opened the shower and took the bottle of wash off the shelf. Kneeling down next the tub, he wet the cloth and poured the fragrant liquid onto it. Soaping it up into a lather, he washed Zandra with a gentleness he didn't know he was capable of, his strength untested on human flesh.

Zandra couldn't find words. She had never had a man take such care with her. Her eyes filled with tears. She had always been a strong, self-sufficient women. She had long ago reassured herself that she didn't need a man to look after her. She found herself humbled by this man, wishing she had met him before the accident. She wanted to know what he looked like. At the moment, he was the most handsome man she had ever met. His behaviour had her drawn to him like a moth to a flame.

"Do you think you can stand if I lift you out?" He needed to get her out of the bath and into his arms. The steady stream of tears was killing him. She nodded, as he scooped her up in his arms and softly placed her feet on the mat.

He leaned over and took the towel from the rack in his hands. He tenderly dried her back and her arms. His breathing became labored as he ran the towel from her neck to her chest. As he lowered the towel to her abdomen, her nipples hardened.

He could do this. He might ache for a week and his balls might turn blue, but he could do this, he reassured himself. His brain repeating the mantra with a towel in either hand, he ventured to her succulent ass at the same time, working towards her pussy. He felt her suddenly steady herself with a hand on his shoulder. He continued down one leg, then back up to her heat. He lingered at her juncture, then down her other leg.

He made the towel into a sarong, "How do you feel?" he asked, while brushing away tears.

"Better, thank you." She moved to the sink and picked up her toothbrush and toothpaste.

"I'm going to organise a cup of tea. I'll

be in the kitchen if you need me." Destiny stepped away from her, needing distance.

He strode into the kitchen and put the kettle on to boil. While he waited, he opened the fridge and took the eggs out. He quickly prepared some scrambled eggs with toast, poured the tea, and was plating up when Zandra made her way to the breakfast bar.

"Wow, something smells good!" she pulled a stool out and sat down.

"Probably only smells good because you haven't eaten anything in days. Give it a try. It's only plain old eggs and toast with a cup of tea." He was praying she would be able to eat some if only a small portion. He silently prayed she would keep it down.

CHAPTER 16

Destiny's time was moving as rapidly as the blink of an eye.

Zandra had become the air he breathed. He loved her with his entire being. He had heard his mother's call to return home, but he wasn't leaving without Zandra.

He spent every waking moment with her. They had been on outings, having dinner together, picnics in the park, and a comedy night at the cafe down the road.

Zandra had not been sick after the first couple of days, so he had no reason to stay in her apartment, no reason to lay with her to sleep. He had tossed and turned with a fever that burned him alive. It had been intense enough that he had stood outside her door several times. He even thought he'd heard her on the other side of the door. When he slept, he dreamed of her, drawing him to her apartment door when he woke. He wanted inside her so badly; he was barely sane.

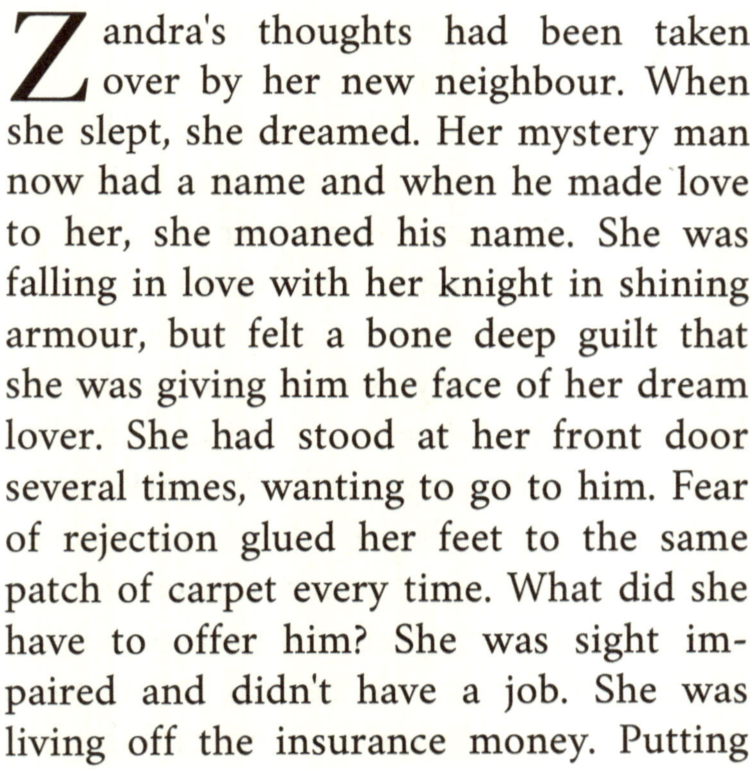

Zandra's thoughts had been taken over by her new neighbour. When she slept, she dreamed. Her mystery man now had a name and when he made love to her, she moaned his name. She was falling in love with her knight in shining armour, but felt a bone deep guilt that she was giving him the face of her dream lover. She had stood at her front door several times, wanting to go to him. Fear of rejection glued her feet to the same patch of carpet every time. What did she have to offer him? She was sight impaired and didn't have a job. She was living off the insurance money. Putting things into perspective was like taking a cold shower.

She climbed out of bed early after another fitful night's sleep. Already having showered and dressed, she sat at the breakfast bar drinking a cup of tea. When she heard a knock, she stood from her seat and moved to open it. As the door swung open, she smelt the waft of Des's cologne and smiled.

Destiny saw red. "I could have been anyone, and you didn't even ask who was there before opening the door." He had her back against the wall, her hands pinned in one of his over her head. His mouth took hers in a crushing tangle of lips and tongue. As she became placid, moaning into his mouth, he gentled. She nipped his bottom lip, the tip of her tongue easing into his mouth. He saw stars, his breathing heavy, as she kissed him back, matching his urgency. As he kicked, the door closed with his boot, she greeted him with a smile. "Good morning to you too," she said.

He took one of her hands in his and led

her to the couch. "I need to ask you something important. My mother just called me. I have to return home. I wish I didn't have to, but it's family business."

Her heart was pounding so loud in her ears, she wasn't sure she was hearing him properly. "When do you leave?" She struggled to get the words past the lump in her throat, she felt like she was going to be sick. "How long will you be gone?"

"I'm asking you to come with me. Before you answer, I need to say, I won't take no for an answer." His lips were on hers before she could form a response. He leaned her back to the cushions and his hardness was pressed against her softness. Her hearing had returned enough to identify the strange sounds around her. She was writhing and panting with the need to have his hands touching her, the noises coming from her throat, just a by-product. She should have been mortified by her actions and response to him, but she'd lost all coherency, all she could do was feel. Her body wanted him more than brain functions.

Her lips were freed from his as he moved to press kisses along her neck. "Yes," was all she could cry as her body came to life, like a bolt of lightning. That's all he needed, all he wanted to hear. He wrapped his arms around Zandra tight. He bit the soft area between her shoulder and neck. She let out a scream as he took her home. The sense of accomplishment overwhelmed him. He was humbled by her choosing him. He took the hem of her shirt in shaking hands, shredding it to reach his prize.

Anyone would think he were a saint for keeping his hands off her all week. He snapped the clasp on her bra, the trapped animal inside him finally roaring with freedom.

He lowered his mouth to her cherry and laved his tongue over it, like he was devouring his favorite fruit. He moved from one to the other, not wanting to miss a single taste. Her keening noises gave him the encouragement. She was enjoying his feast just as much as he was.

He slid down her body, as he positioned himself for dessert, lifting her skirt to her waist. He guided her legs apart as his hands stroked down from her knees, along her inner thighs. She gasped breathlessly as he tore her panties off. Tossing them aside, he lowered to swipe his parched tongue along her slippery entrance.

His thumbs opened her up for his unwavering attention. His tongue plundered her deeply, her hips rising to meet the building need. His thumb finding her clit, he circled it, driving her pleasure higher. The edge of the cliff was within reach, he held her there. Unable to catch a breath, her throat was on fire, her lungs burning. He replaced his tongue first with one finger, then two. Curling their tips to play over a delicate spot, her inner muscles tightened. She couldn't take much more, squirming for purchase. His mouth covering her swollen nub, his tongue applied pressure. As he suckled the exposed head, she exploded. Juices flowed over his fingers. He moaned, sending vibrations through her already pulsing clit. Her inner muscles convulsing, he wrung another orgasm to life before the first had subsided.

He reared up, snapping the button on his jeans, tearing the zipper open. His throbbing cock sprang free, and he paused, holding himself steady at her entrance. Leaning down to her, he kissed her, thrusting his tongue into her mouth. He buried himself so deep, he couldn't tell where she began or he ended. He was complete, home at last. That's when he started to move, "I can't be gentle. I've needed this for too long," he warned her.

"Then don't hold back. I think I can handle it." Her lips pressed against his throat. Her hand in his hair, she bit him. He lifted her leg higher as he started hammering over-sensitive nerves at the entry to her womb. Her muscles clamped down around him like a velvet fist. Her nails dug into the flesh of his ass, spurring him on. He lifted his head and with one last thrust, he roared his release, her back bowed and her hips tilted, as her own orgasm ground through every particle of her being. They collapsed in a spent heap, sated, exhausted, well-loved up, gasping for air.

Destiny pushed himself up, not wanting to crush her with his significant size. He pulled her onto his lap, hand reached over to the lamp on the side table.

CHAPTER 17

She fell off his lap as she scrambled away from him. Her eyes wide, she fought to find her footing. Her knees failed to hold her, and she sprawled unceremoniously on her ass. "What the fuck!" she exclaimed, as she crawled backwards out of his reach.

For a split second she thought she had fallen asleep after having the most gratifyingly orgasmic sex of her entire life, except as she looked around, she was no longer in her apartment, but surrounded by all things dream lover. Had she really hit her head on something? Her eyes settled on her mystery lover, "Who the fuck are you and what did you do with Des?"

Destiny ran his hand through his hair. As his hand passed, he could smell her on his skin, taste her on his lips. "Zandra, I am Des," his voice sounding like she had bitch-slapped him, his expression showing she'd struck him where it hurts. "Des is short for Destiny."

Realisation struck as the room's appearance registered. She'd been here before. Had he drugged her before bringing her here? She didn't even know where here was. How would she get home? He'd kidnapped her. Nobody knew she was gone, they wouldn't know where to find her.

"What kind of trick is this? I don't understand. I've seen this place before." Her mind was running so fast she couldn't keep up. She pulled her knees up to her chin and started rocking. After a brief moment of contemplation, she raised herself of the floor, walked toward her captor and slapped his face. How dare he think he could do this to her! She trusted him. Damn it she was falling in love with him. She needed to find her way out of this mind fuck, so she ran, not knowing how long she would be able to see.

Destiny tucked himself in. Okay, so he hadn't handled things very well. He hadn't had much, if any, interaction with humans. He had no idea how to go about explaining the situation at hand. He was about to try when his cheek lit up like a struck match.

As he reached out for Zandra, his hands met empty space. She was gone, running. He let her go. He couldn't force her to listen to his pathetic excuses. She had to process her surroundings and calm down first, then he would talk to her and explain everything.

In the meantime, he now had a name. He sighed as he started his search of the library shelves. He needed to find Zandra's volume on the shelf. It may hold some an-swers or the key to how he was going to fix things.

❧

Zandra ran out of the library. The first door she found was open and led to a bedroom with an all too familiar king sized bed. Her memory of the room played scenes, unsure if they were real or dreams. She wasn't ready to cross that threshold, so she ventured further toward the door at the end of the hall, hoping it would lead to the outside and not further into a night-mare or dream or whatever the hell was going on here.

She found the door unlocked, so she opened it to find the area dark. She moved through the doorway looking over her shoulder to see if he was following her. Quietly she pulled the door shut to avoid his detection. The space around her was so dark it was like she was standing in a black hole, probably a broom closet, knowing her luck. As she felt along the wall for a light switch, she found the walls were curved and had doorknobs every couple of feet. She tried the first door to the left and found it locked, so moved to the next. It too was locked, the next one after wasn't. She took a calming breath and tried to re-assure herself that it wouldn't lead her back to the library and the man she was trying to avoid.

As she opened the door, it looked at first like the hall she had just left. However it wasn't, it felt different, unstable. She giggled quietly to herself, SHE was unstable! She tiptoed down the hall, listening for movements. As she stood at a doorway to what would be a library, she peeked around the timber frame. What the fuck? Inside the room was a large-scale map of the world, like an atlas but the size of an Olympic swimming pool. Confused and curious, she snuck into the room for a closer look. There were all manner of objects laid out, some were symbols made of brass. Some areas had glasses of water, some piles of sand. What the hell sort of game was this?

Her hand was itching to touch and looking around she couldn't see anyone. She picked up one of the amulets and placed it in her pocket. She would ask Des about it later with all the other questions she had. She heard a noise from down the other end of the hall and froze, listening. With the weight of the object in her pocket, weighing heavily on her mind, she needed to get out of here before someone found her. Moving back to the door leading to the hall, her back settled on the wall. Carefully she peered around the frame. She saw an enormous leather clad warrior, very similar in features to Des, but bigger. His shit kickers eating up the distance with long strides, she whispered under her breath, "Crap!" He was bound to find her. She needed a place to hide, and fast.

Destruction entered the room, plate in one hand, bottle in another. Taking a swig of his beer, he washed his roast beef sandwich down. He paused. Something was different. He ran his eye over each continent, there was something not right. He put his beer down in the Pacific Ocean. Yeah, scientists would be recording an increase in sea levels right about now and reports of global warming would be the news headlines. Who was he to care? Humans constantly raped and pillaged their environment. A little fear never hurt anyone. Serve them right for wiping out so much of the Rain Forests. Zandra was watching from behind the door. The big guy was busy scrutinizing the map in front of him. He was clenching his fists, his body tense as if he knew something was missing. Sliding carefully around the door, she ran down the hall to where she had entered. Turning the knob she opened it and stole back into the dark abyss. She closed it as quietly as possible, not wanting to alert anyone to her intrusion.

Zandra opened the third door back on the right. She peeked to see if the coast was clear. With no sight of Des, she stepped through, turned and was headed back to the library.

She still couldn't see Des anywhere as she stood in the doorway. Maybe he had left, gone somewhere. She was just tossing around in her head if she wanted to search for him in hope of some answers, when a gale blew open the end door, followed by an enormous shit kicker. "Crap!" she recognised the boot and its wearer, "Okay, this can't be good!" she muttered.

Every step taken left a fracture in the tiles, the door left with splinters in the timber from where he had touched it to close it behind his enormous body.

"Destiny, where are you?" he bellowed, the wall vibrating with the force of the tone he used. He stopped halfway down the hall. Staring at her, she felt all the colour drain from her face. Her knees threatened to give way as one hand went to her pocket, and the other to her stomach, she felt nauseous. She turned and ran for the bedroom's bathroom, as Destiny appeared a few feet away from the big guy.

Destiny felt his brother's presence as he

entered his realm, now was not a good time. He'd spent the last hour feeling the spine of every journal in the library where Zandra's should have been. His head was hurting from it, and he still couldn't understand why he hadn't been able to locate it.

With his hearing intensified to compensate for his lack of sight, he could hear Zandra being sick in his bathroom. He needed to get to her. His protective instincts overrode everything else. He ordered his brother to stay where he was. He'd deal with him after he saw to Zandra.

He entered the bathroom, opened the cupboard under the sink and grabbed a washcloth. Soaking it with cold water, he wrung it out and carefully moved to the side of the tub. Sitting down, he put his hand out to feel for his female. He found her lying on the cool tiles near the toilet. "Baby, I can't see you." This was one of those times he despised being blind. His woman needed him and he couldn't see her to know if she was all right. He knew her eyes were closed as his mind's eye was filled with darkness. He carefully positioned himself behind her as he lifted her into his arms and gently carried her to the bed. He laid her down, his hand on her face, and he cleaned her of any remnants. After returning from the bathroom where he acquired a fresh cloth, he folded it and placed it on her forehead. As he drew his hands away, Zandra grabbed his hand and whispered, "Thank you." Through her scorched throat, she hadn't opened her eyes. She could feel the big warrior watching her, and she was not ready to feel the guilt from what she'd taken from him.

Destruction stood at the door to his brother's bedroom, watching. He was puzzled as to who the woman now lying in Destiny's bed was and confused as to what was wrong with her.

He leaned his shoulder against the frame and heard it crack. Looking at it sideways, he knew he should have known better than to touch anything outside his own realm. The only place safe for him was in his realm. The minute he touched

anything outside, things got wrecked, ru-
ined and destroyed.

"Destiny, man I need a word and it's urgent," he said, noting that he didn't have
time to waste. He needed to find the
amulet.

CHAPTER 18

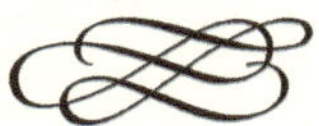

Destiny leaned down and placed a kiss on Zandra's cheek, "I have to see what my brother needs and then I'll be back to check on you, okay."

So the big guy was his brother, she had seen the resemblance. She nodded, "Hmhm. I'm not going anywhere. I feel like absolute crap. I could do with a little water when you come back if it's not too much bother?"

Destiny pushed past his brother on his way to the kitchen for a glass of cold water. He snarled, "I thought I told you to stay where you were?"

Destruction ignored his brother, continuing to lean against the frame. While observing the female in his brother's room, he found himself feeling envious of the connection that seemed to be happening between his brother and this female. He hadn't wanted for anything before now, but he wanted to feel the softness of a women's skin under his touch. He shook his head. That was just a wishful, stupid thought. He destroyed everything with a touch from his little finger. He couldn't hope for things he couldn't have. It left him cold on the inside at the thought of what he would never know. His brother's return brought him out of his dark depressing thoughts as he pushed past.

Destiny sat on the edge of the bed, helping the female to rise enough to take a few swallows of water. Placing the glass on the table beside the bed, he pulled the comforter over her telling her to rest, he would be back soon. He removed the washcloth from her forehead to replace it with his lips for a brief moment.

Destruction's teeth now grinding with jealousy, he growled and pushed away from the door in disgust. Not for his brother and his actions, but for himself. He stormed into Destiny's library and stood looking at what resembled the aftermath of a tornado. There were journals thrown all over the floor, the desk, the couch. What the fuck happened in here?

Destiny stormed into the room on the heels of Destruction. "What do you want? Why are you here?"

Destruction countered with his own set of questions, "What happened in here? And who is the women? Where did you find her?"

Destiny pointed out, "I asked first. You came to me." Wow, even he knew it sounded childish.

Destruction, turned with a snarl on his face. His brother may be blind but he knew it would resonate through his voice as he said, "Someone has taken one of my amulets. I'm guessing since everyone knows of their importance and their dangers it's not one of us. I came here as your realm is the only door unlocked at present."

He continued, "As you know, I can sense their energy, and I felt it the minute I walked in. Who is the female? Where did she come from?"

Destiny ran his hand through his hair. Where did he start? He just blurted it out, "She's my mate, my female. She's here because I manipulated the situation and brought her here. I've been searching for her journal, but can't find it."

Destruction was too dumbfounded to speak after hearing the bombshell his brother had just confessed. Wait, he needed to know how he had discovered he had a female in the first place. How did she had come to be in Destiny's realm?

Destiny explained all that had transpired over the last few weeks, all of it. He didn't leave anything out, including how Death's friend, Vanessa had helped find Zandra in the human realm.

Destruction's gut was telling him that maybe there was a female for him. His head was laughing at him saying not a chance. However, the seed of hope had been planted.

He started to leave as he was feeling anxious and unsettled. His mind had become unfocused as to his reason for being in Destiny's library. The amulet! He'd almost forgotten it.

Destruction sighed, "I am happy for you brother, but I came hoping you could help me. One of my amulets has been taken and I need it back. It's here somewhere. I felt it close by when I was approaching your female. I believe she may have it or know where it is."

Destiny frowned, "I guess we will have to ask her. Follow me. I don't understand if she has it, how she managed to leave my realm and enter yours completely undetected by the both of us. She shouldn't have been able to leave my realm without me sensing it. Maybe I was just too preoccupied with my search."

⁓

Zandra was resting peacefully as Destiny entered the bedroom. He sat beside her on the bed. He didn't want to disturb her, but if she had managed to acquire Destruction's emblem, they needed to know how.

Destruction couldn't understand how the human was still alive. The emblem, if touched by anyone other than a god or goddess, would suffer its benediction.

The one that Destiny's female had taken was Cholera. The onset would have been instant. As a human she would already be showing signs and symptoms. Even more so, he thought, as Destiny said his female was already ill.

Destruction started to think that maybe they should call for their mother. She would be the only one who could fix this. He expressed his concerns to Destiny, "We need to speak to mother. She'll know what to do. Your woman has been exposed to Cholera. She could die if we don't."

Without stalling, Destiny and Destruction called out, "Mother."

Cosmo appeared beside her son, Destruction. She had heard the distressed tone in both her sons' voices. Looking from one to the other, she asked, "What worries my two sons this day?"

Destruction explained that somehow Destiny's female had entered his realm and taken the emblem representing Cholera. He said that he could feel the symbol's hum, coming from the female's direction in the room. He also needed it back before the loss of the emblem from its mark changed the course of events in South America.

Cosmo rolled her eyes at her serious son Destruction, "You need to lighten up some. You're always so serious. Not everything has to be so melodramatic. The girl will be fine," she said as she took the emblem from Zandra's pocket. She issued calming words to Destiny's female as she stirred, "It's all right dear you go back to sleep. I'll take care of this." Zandra rolled to her side, but didn't rouse enough to fully awaken. Cosmo passed the emblem back to her son, Destruction. With a warning to take better care next time to lock his realm's door to avoid things like this happening again, she dismissed him.

Destruction took his mother's lead and left. He needed to return to his realm to restore the balance. Walking down the hall, he left his brother's realm, closing the door behind him.

Zandra opened her eyes to see a beautiful women standing behind Destiny, there were some similarities. This woman had to be another of Destiny's relatives. The women looked at her with a slight curve to her mouth as if she knew more than she should.

Zandra's hand went to her pocket, feeling for the trinket she had placed there. It was gone, but the memory of it was still ripe. She knew someone had taken it, probably the big warrior. She worried her bottom lip under the scrutiny of the women standing in the room. She felt self-conscious, like she didn't belong here.

She sat up gingerly, swinging her legs over the side of bed. She steadied herself before standing up. Destiny moved faster than her eye could see, to place an arm around her waist.

"Mother, this is Zandra. She is my chosen female. Zandra, this is Cosmo, my mother." Introductions aside, she felt as if she were being judged by his mother. She wasn't intimidated by her, she just didn't like that curve of her lips.

Cosmo stood there summing up her son's chosen in her mind. She knew every detail of this women's life. She'd read every page of her journal, watched her grow, seen her mistakes and knew that her son was not going to be in for an easy life, now that he had her here with him. However, she looked upon them with a sense of the unknown. It sparked in her a little fear for her son, but there was no going back now.

"You must be more careful in the future not to take the toys of others from the sandpit. It could be dangerous to your health. If not for the life you carry, you most likely would be dead now," Cosmo warned.

"Mother, I love you but I will not allow you to threaten what's mine." Destiny stepped in front of Zandra offering his protection.

"Destiny I want to go home now," she said, hoping that it was just that easy, although in her mind, she knew this was more than just a dream she could wake up from.

CHAPTER 19

Cosmo laughed, and with a flurry of movement she swept out of her son's bedroom. She was not going to discuss things in there.

She walked across the hall to the study, to find the room ransacked. Sighing, she waved both hands in a pattern to dismiss the mess. All of the journals disappeared from the floor to reappear in order on the shelves. With a hmm of satisfaction she walked to Destiny's desk and sat down. There she waited.

estiny wrapped his arms around Zandra. He lowered his cheek to rest on the top of her head. Guilt racked him to the core. He loved her, but he couldn't let her go. If she left, he would follow. He would walk away from his family, his duty. He would be human for her.

He was pissed at himself for presuming that she would do the same for him. He hadn't given her a choice. He now realised he was no longer in charge of his own fate. It all rested in the small, delicate hands of Zandra. However, he was willing to take that risk. Lifting his head to place a kiss on Zandra's forehead, he whispered, "My mother is waiting in the study. We need to listen to what she has to say and I need to speak to her about getting you home." He took her hand and made a remark about it not being wise to keep her waiting if things were going to be in their favour.

Zandra followed him into the study. Dropping his hand, she moved to sit on the couch with her hands folded in her lap. Destiny moved to sit beside Zandra. He wasn't about to let his mother intimidate Zandra. They would present as a united front, even if Zandra didn't want him after the mess he'd made of things.

He'd been selfish, and he wouldn't promise that would change when it came to Zandra. When it came to her, he couldn't think straight. It was like his brain short circuited.

She was his calm to his inner storm. She diffused the ticking time bomb in his head.

~

Zandra didn't have a clue about any of this. It was like she had fallen down the rabbit hole and was now trapped in some surreal Alice in Wonderland nightmare. She just wanted black and white answers about what was going on.

Destiny reached over, took one of her fidgeting hands from her lap and squeezed it. She knew in that breath, she must be bat-shit crazy, delusional, and needed to be signed up for a padded cell, loopy.

Zandra knew she needed to keep her head screwed on straight or she would start screaming from fear for her own sanity.

The conflicting emotions did not however, dampen her feelings for the man holding her hand, sitting beside her.

She needed to think. She needed answers and a plan which she could handle, though not when Destiny was so close or touching her. His scent left her oblivious and unable to think. Fear of the unknown stopped her from letting him go, so she stayed there seated on the couch.

She had to admit he had become the air she breathed, the comforting touch she craved, and the beat of her heart. He was her knight in shining armour and her dream lover.

Cosmo had sat there long enough. She had watched them as they joined hands, presenting as one. She stood while speaking to her son, "I'm glad to have you back in the fold. I grow tiresome of your duties along with my own. How is Zandra holding up through all of this?" she asked as she rounded the oversized desk.

Destiny stiffened as Zandra's hand tightened in his hold. She stood, to match the height of his mother. She would not be spoken down to, or allow Destiny to speak for her. Destiny stiffened at Zandra's answering tone, "I AM in the room. I can hear you and I have a tongue. I can speak for myself."

Cosmo smiled, "I think I like you already." She took Zandra's hand in hers. She placed a small box in her hand. "Yes, you will be good for my son, you will teach him much. He will now have a renewed way of performing his duties. When you are ready to face the unknown, you should open it."

Zandra stammered, "I can't stay here. I have a life back at home."

Cosmo frowned, "I'm sorry dear, but you can't leave. Not before you birth my first grandchild, after which, you are free to leave if you are still inclined to do so.

You can return the box unopened if you choose to leave. If you open it before then, you will seal your fate." Cosmo held her hand palm up offering Zandra a small, intricately carved cube.

For a second Zandra stood there eyeing the beautiful craftsmanship, it was exquisite. Her thoughts cleared as she shook her head. "I'm sorry, what did you say?" She couldn't breathe. It sounded like she was telling Zandra she was pregnant.

Cosmo smiled wickedly at them both, "I wouldn't allow my Destiny's fate to set course without a backup plan. I am the creator of new life. Your destiny is my son's, and his destiny is you. Now my grandchild's destiny depends on the both of you. You will give birth to the next generation, in just less than eight months, enough time for the two of you to get your shit together."

Zandra looked from Destiny to the couch they had been together on a short while ago. They'd had mind blowing, unprotected sex right there. When she looked back at Cosmo, she was shaking her head with a knowing glint in her eye. "My grandchild was not conceived this day, but was created the first time you were together. I call it grandmother's insurance."

Cosmo paused for only a second before continuing. "Know that while you are here in the realm of Destiny, you have the gift of sight. If you return to your home, you return to the sightless world my son lives in here. You have many things to think about. I'll leave now, but when you decide your path, I will return. Destiny can reach out to me." With that Cosmo vanished, the tiny box left sitting on the floor where she had been. Zandra reached down, picked it up and sat it on the desk in front of her. As she went to let her fingers go, she paused. It was like it was a part of her. Instead, she tightened her hold and lifted it to her pocket. She didn't trust leaving it for anyone to find. She needed to protect it.

Zandra was swung around and pulled up against Destiny's hard chest. He sank to his knees and placed his forehead to her belly. She moved away, "Your mother is a manipulative bitch! How dare she? What gives her the right to do all this?"

He tried to touch her, but she stepped back. "I can't do this. I need to go home." She stormed out of the room. As she reached the bedroom, she looked over her shoulder. 'Great! Now I'm a thirty something year old brat.'

She purposely walked into the bathroom and slammed the door, locking it. After washing her face with cold water, she tied her hair back into a knot. Opening the door, she ran to the bed, throwing herself down and proceeding to cry tears of anger and frustration. Wonderful. She cried even harder because she hated crying.

Destiny knew he could make this right, he had too. It was like one of his brothers had punched him in the chest but more. The ache was bone deep, he could hear her sadness. He walked to his desk, opened the bottom drawer and took out a bottle scotch. Uncorking it, he lifted it to his lips taking three hard pulls and a slow breath intake to ease the after burn. He pushed the cork into the bottle and slammed it on his desk. 'Fuck this!' he thought I will not be pushed away. He just had to find a way to convince her to choose him. Starting right fucking now!

He stormed into the bedroom to find Zandra curled up on her side. He eased his big body down beside her. He gently wrapped around her. Placing his hand and spreading it on her stomach, he kissed the back of her neck. He whispered softly, "I'm home as long as you're in my arms, and I plan to keep you." He relaxed and fell asleep.

She woke tucked into a warm, hard body. She didn't want to admit that she felt like she was home.

What she wanted to focus on was where the hell her book was in the library. She needed to know if she could find and change it. Before she could move, Destiny stirred beside her. She held her breath, hoping he would relinquish his hold on her. Nope, not going to happen. She felt his embrace tighten. She squirmed, pushing her hip into the bed so as to roll over, but all it seemed to do was nudge Destiny's growing hardness more firmly against her ass.

CHAPTER 20

Laying there trying to work out what to do, her eyes settled on the intricate box resting on the bedside table. She wanted to know what was inside it. Her fingers were itching to open it. One of her many faults was her unbearable curiosity. She always needed to know about the missing puzzle piece, always needing the answer to the bigger picture. She growled low in her throat with the temptation.

With her eyes wide, her back hit the mattress, her legs spread wide. Destiny was leaning over her. A concerned frown moulded his brow. He inquired, "Are you unwell? What do you need me to do?" Her breath stuttered. Her heart and her body knew what they wanted and at the moment they were not listening to her head. She felt moisture pool between her folds, as her body and mind battled over the growing awareness that she would love to spend the rest of her days underneath, on top of, wrapped around and wrapped up by, this man.

An unconscious roll of her hips had Destiny's hardness nestled along the seam of her wetted lips. Zandra whimpered, her body ached and the fire of desire had been lit. She opened her eyes and placed her hands on either side of his face, drawing him down. He felt the slightest brush of Zandra's lips against his. He needed her like his next breath, but he stilled, letting her come to him instead of him chasing her.

She tested his patience with the tip of her tongue, then nipped his bottom lip. He opened his mouth for her and met her tongue in a slow dance. Her kiss became more urgent, begging for his response. He returned the depth of her passion tenfold, both of them breathing heavily with need, he rolled to his back taking her with him.

Zandra pushed herself up, a knee to either side of his hips. She needed him so badly. She ached to be filled, stretched. She lifted the hem of her commandeered shirt up over her head, tossing it to the side of the bed.

She leaned forward to kiss Destiny again. She wanted to feel skin to skin with him. Her nipples pebbled the moment their flesh met. His body was hot to the touch, with smooth ridges. Her lips lifted from his, and working little nips and kisses along his jaw, she sucked his earlobe. She was burning alive, the fire of desire so intense she could no longer think. Running her tongue down his neck to his nipple, she circled it before gently playing her teeth over its budding hardness. Destiny moaned, lifting his hips toward her aching snatch. With Destiny's meager encouragement she lowered down to remove his sweats, tossing them to the floor at the foot of the bed. She prowled back up his body to lick the length of his throbbing cock. Destiny's thighs lifted from the bed to prompt for her purchase. Her tongue lapped over his weeping crown. His breath released on a low growl. She was pushing to the very edge of his control. His determination to let her have this time to explore him, was fighting his need to dominate. He was burning up with the need to be buried deep inside his female.

Zandra climbed up to straddle Destiny. Shifting, she turned to plant her right foot beside Destiny's right hip weaving her left leg under his left thigh. Her right hand circled his cock, raising it to the dripping mouth of her pussy, with the head nestled just right. Destiny's hands reached for her hips as she impaled herself in one swift motion. Her muscles pulsed around him as the head bumped her cervix. She moaned, while Destiny took long deep breaths to stop himself from exploding instantly.

After allowing her body to stretch and relax around the size of her man, she started to move, reverse cowgirl, riding side-saddle. Destiny raised his right leg slightly to allow him to meet her downward glides. Zandra placed a hand behind her in the centre of Destiny's chest, leaning for balance, as she increased the speed from a stroll to a gallop. The increasing friction ran the race to the finish line. Destiny's control finally snapped. He grabbed Zandra's wrist from his chest and lifting to press his chest to her back, he wrapped his arm around Zandra to take both her wrists in his left hand.

His right hand kneaded her right breast, teasing her nipple, plucking it. Zandra whimpered as her head fell back onto Destiny's shoulder, his hot tongue and lips instantly fuelling her need as he nibbled her neck. His hand lowered to toy with her already over-sensitive clit. She saw stars behind her closed eyelids. What was he trying to do to her, give her a stroke? Struggling for breath, she needed more... more something, she didn't know. Too confused and caught up in the moment, all she could do was beg, "More, I can't." With all control gone, Destiny rolled sideways with his arms around Zandra. Lifting him with her, he raised himself to his knees, hands moving to her hips, she followed.

He placed one hand in the middle of her back leaving one hand on her hip. He settled, and taking a deep breath, he slowly reseated himself. Zandra hummed. He reversed to his tip just as slowly, testing the angle. He was rewarded with the sound of Zandra's needy whimper. "Don't move," he ordered, "I'll take care of you. I'll always take care of you baby." His hand slid down her back to circle her ass cheek twice before he swatted it. He rammed hard and fast, balls deep inside her. He was determined to teach her that he knew how to master her body. She pushed back and rolled her hips with a groan. He again withdrew to the tip with a slow drawn breath. Lowering his chest to meet Zandra's back, he braced one hand beside her on the bed as his other hand made playtime with her engorged clit.

His rhythm started to pound deep inside her channel while he rolled his fingers. Zandra's eyes were scrunched, closed tight, the sensation too intense. Her body was rocking to Destiny's rhythm. Unable to recognize if it was his song or hers, she was screaming along to their song, their sounds of moans and groans, growls and screams as they both slammed over the edge free falling to ecstasy. Destiny lost his load the second Zandra's sweet tight pussy started to squeeze him with strangling strength. He buried deep with his last ounce of stamina, emptying his balls. After struggling to catch his breath for several minutes, he placed a kiss between her shoulder blades as he scooped her up and rolled to his side. He tucked her into the confines of his body. He kissed her shoulder saying, "I love you."

She opened her eyes to find the tiny box staring at her. Destiny could see the box on the bedside table through Zandra's eyes. He wished he could tell what she was thinking.

Zandra's words were just above a whisper, "What do you suppose is in the box Cosmo gave me?"

He replied, "Honestly, I wouldn't have a clue. I know the box itself is what my brother keeps the souls in once he retrieves them."

Zandra stiffened, "So that box could be the one my soul is placed in when I die. Why would she give me that? She said when I made my choice to open it. I've made my decision but I'm scared to see what's inside."

Destiny held his breath. She had come to some resolve about staying or going, her destiny wasn't his to choose. He needed to know. He'd go crazy if he kept trying to second guess himself. He hoped he'd done enough to sway her, if his love was enough to keep her. "Are you going to let me in on what your plan is?" he asked.

Zandra replied flatly, "No." She stretched, climbing off the bed and away from Destiny. "I'm going to have a shower and while I do that I need you to call Cosmo. I think she can meet me in the study. I'll be about ten minutes."

She would have had to hold back the smile longer as she walked into the bathroom, but he couldn't see her face. He would have heard her laugh at the look on his face as she answered him though. It was priceless.

She knew it was unfair to Destiny, but it was about time someone taught Cosmo she would not be manipulated again, even if it was for her son's sake. Cosmo had taken away her free will, her freedom to choose for herself.

She was not about to admit that she'd had time to think about everything and she had a plan that would get what she wanted. It would be all in her favour, at the end of the day.

CHAPTER 21

As Zandra entered Destiny's study, she acknowledged Cosmo with the tilt of her head. The goddess did not look happy about being here, but she'd bet her last dollar that the look would be worse by the time she finished this little discussion. She was taking hold of her destiny with both hands.

"I need to know first up if I can speak freely without some kind of goddess backlash?" she started. There was no need for bad mojo following her around, no matter what her brain decided to let loose from her mouth.

Cosmo looked from Zandra to Destiny

and back again, fists clenched. On a hiss she responded, "No my dear. There will be no repercussions for what you're about to say. After all you're the mother of my grandchild." She looked pissed from the implication, but Zandra was being careful. She wasn't here for warm fuzzies, she was here for business.

"Alright then," Zandra replied.

~

7 & 1/2 Months Later

Zandra's back had been aching all day, but she was satisfied with the additional touches to the nursery.

She could not believe that Cosmo had come to the party on all her conditions and had even added a few perks herself. Zandra could tell that it was purely a mother's love for her son that had been the driving force.

Destiny's realm had been anchored to a

small Island off the Gold Coast, in sunny Queensland, Australia. Sovereign Island housed some of the most beautiful mansions, allowing theirs to just blend in unremarkably. It was only accessible via a short drive over the secured bridge to the mainland, meaning she was able to stay in contact with her best friend JT. Although JT had been confused about the whole thing, she hadn't argued. She could tell they were happy.

She found herself spinning the eternity ring on her left hand. Destiny had placed it there following the scene in the study. She smiled, recalling the intricate box. She was now one of them. As long as she kept the ring on her finger, she would live forever. Yes, they would probably have to relocate to different parts of the country to avoid suspicion, but that was a small price to pay.

Cosmo had held up all of her end of the bargain. Destiny's warmth wrapped around her as his arms circled her waist, his hands splayed on either side of her swollen belly. "Relax baby, everything is going to be just fine," he whispered in her ear, before sucking it between his lips. Her womb contracted, "Hey, that's not funny." She slapped the back of his hand while breathing heavy, to get past the spasm.

She smiled, thinking how Cosmo had implemented one of her own conditions that day. Zandra was grateful to her mother-in-law. She had granted her son's eyes the gift of sight. Destiny would be able to watch and see first-hand the birth of their child. The only time he couldn't see, was the minute he walked into his study to resume his duties. However, that meant he could see the beautiful view from the bedroom balcony that over-looked the white beaches curving around their home. They often made love on that balcony to the rhythm of the waves pounding the sand. Things could not have been a more perfect fit.

At first, Destiny had been overly pissed at his mother for not gifting him sooner. With time, he had forgiven her, as Cosmo had gone out of her way to make amends.

They were now together and living in a

home filled with love. Cosmo took the time to visit regularly. On her first visit to their home she had brought a house warming gift. She had been keeping Zandra and Destiny's books on a shelf in her locked library.

Cosmo appeared from nowhere saying, "It's time! I've called for Death to bring Vanessa. She will be here in minutes," as all of a sudden Zandra felt like she had peed herself. 'How embarrassing, and I really liked these shoes.' Her contractions came on strongly within minutes. Okay, she so didn't want to do this shit anymore. Destiny lifted her into his arms and moved her to the spare room they had set it up ready for this precise moment only a couple of days ago.

Destiny helped Zandra undress in the attached bathroom and turned on the shower. He helped her get in after stripping his jeans and T-shirt off. He helped her to stand up, while circling the hot water over her lower back and then her stomach, back, stomach. After ten minutes, Zandra whimpered in mid-contraction, shaking her head from side to side. He turned off the water quickly, wrapped her in a king sized towel and lifted her up to carry her to the bed, oblivious to the fact he was naked in front of his mother, his brother Death and Vanessa.

"Dude, put some clothes on!" his brother's voice sounded harsh.

Destiny noticed at a glance that his brother was watching Vanessa in an over possessive way, even though Vanessa was oblivious to anything in the room except Zandra.

Vanessa was checking blood pressure and listening to heart beats with a fetal monitor. Counting contractions and timing them. He was completely devoted to his female's well-being. As he grabbed sweat pants and shoved them on, he turned to his brother. "You need to leave! You can wait out there somewhere."

Death was pacing back and forth along the hall. At least Vanessa had stayed put this time, but for how long? He had his suspicions that once Destiny's female was taken care of that she would once again up and flee. After hundreds of years, he was getting tired of her running and hiding every time she sensed him. He needed to get this shit sorted. Trapped in his own thoughts for God only knew how long, the sound of a baby's cry pulled him back to the here and now with a spark of jealousy.

Zandra leaned back in exhaustion, thinking she'd be damned if she was going to do this again. She would have to speak to Cosmo about messing with her birth control.

The little bundle was wrapped in a warm blanket and passed to Zandra. Looking down she asked, "So little one what are we going to call you?"

Cosmo stepped forward, bent to one knee before her grandchild, bowed her head, kissed her fingertips and placed them on the baby's forehead, "I would be honoured if you would name her Iva. It means life. One day when she is much older and possesses the wisdom, it will be her turn to be the spinner of life." She stood with grace and retreated after adding, "Zandra, I owe you much. The gift you have given me today is priceless. I would never have dreamed that I would bear witness to the birth of my first grandchild. The joy I find is overwhelming. I shall leave you now, but if you need anything, anything at all just call. I will be here in the same breath."

Zandra turned to Destiny with a raised eyebrow, "Well that was intense. So what do you think of the name Iva? I think it sounds kind of funny, when you think Iva Chancellor, but we could go with Iva Wilson-Chancellor."

Destiny just sat there with the biggest, most stupid grin on his face. She raised her right hand from the cheek of her daughter to the face of the man she loved and adored. She smiled back then giggled, "Baby is you in there somewhere? Just breathe. I think you're in shock."

Destiny could not stop smiling. He had captured the heart of the women he loved. After what he'd seen her go through today, hell, he fucking worshipped her. He was a daddy to the most perfect little baby girl he'd ever seen. He started laughing. Okay so now he probably looked like he was losing it, but his world had just been made perfect. "Private joke, I'll tell you later," he said as he slid his gaze to Vanessa.

Vanessa finished cleaning everything up. She removed the rubber gloves from her hands adding them to the bio-hazard bag. She turned as Destiny approached. He raised his hand and gave her an amulet on a piece of leather strand. Smiling he said, "I can't thank you enough. If you ever need anything, hold this in your hand and call my name. I will be there, night or day."

She nodded her head and placed it around her neck saying, "I will, thanks. I'm done here, so I guess I'll be on my way.

Offer stands for you guys too, if you need anything, well here's my number." Destiny placed the piece of paper in his pocket. He'd add it to his phone later.

Vanessa took one last look over her shoulder, with envy for the happy new family. She left to find Death. He would take her home.....

ABOUT THE AUTHOR

Melissa Bell is a USA Today Best Selling Author who lives in Brisbane, Australia. At a point in her life where she felt she needed something just for herself, she discovered the pleasures of writing. Her most frequently used comment to herself is there's not enough time in a day. She enjoys good food and good company, when she's not trying to concentrate on her writing. She also loves to laugh and most of the time, she cracks herself up. She is hoping that this is the start of something amazing and one day aspires to be listed amongst those blessed with the title of being on the New York Times Best Sellers list.

When she isn't writing she loves to read, many of which she has read over and over again while listening to her favorite

Australian bands - Birds of Tokyo and Karnivool.

Please keep an eye out for other books by Melissa Bell.

Stay safe and thank you for reading my book.

Dutiful Gods Series

Book #1 Destiny's Fate

Book #2 Taming Destruction

Book #3 Morpheus's Dream

Book #4 Defying Death

Book #5 Cosmo (TBA)

Five Brothers Series

Book#1 Houston

Book#2 Felan

Book#3 Tate

Book #4 Channon

Book #4.5 Lupe

(First story in 'Compilation'- A Collection of Short Stories)

Book #5 London

Books still to come in this series include –

Blaez and Brody amongst others.

(So stay tuned)